She laughed. H
he'd never kisse
And she lifted
her neck just a little bit farther,
enough so that she could look him
in the eye as she gave him
the most precious gift imaginable.

"I love you," she said. "You have no idea how much I love you."

That was it. Overcome, he caught her face in his hand and kissed her. Her mouth was slick and minty, her tongue eager. She opened for him, mewling with pleasure, and he marveled at all the infinite ways their lips could fit together.

Soon the sucking turned to nipping, the nipping to biting, and before he knew it, he was filling his hands with her soft breasts and shaking with urgency.

Breathing was all but impossible.

They broke apart, panting.

Her lips were swollen and wet now, her eyes feverish with need. He knew the feeling. It amazed him that he'd had anything to do with making her burn so hot that her body nearly singed his palms. And Sandro couldn't get enough of her.

She paused. Focused. "Please tell me you're not going to regret this tomorrow."

"There's no way in hell."

Books by Ann Christopher

Kimani Romance

Just About Sex
Sweeter Than Revenge
Tender Secrets
Road to Seduction
Campaign for Seduction
Redemption's Kiss
Seduced on the Red Carpet
Redemption's Touch
The Surgeon's Secret Baby
Sinful Seduction

ANN CHRISTOPHER

is a full-time chauffeur for her two overscheduled children. She is also a wife, former lawyer and decent cook. In between trips to various sporting practices and games, Target and the grocery store, she likes to write the occasional romance novel. She lives in Cincinnati and spends her time with her family, which includes two spoiled rescue cats, Sadie and Savannah, and two rescue hounds, Sheldon and Dexter. Her next book for Harlequin/Kimani Press, *Sinful Temptation*, which is part of her Twins of Sin series, will be a March 2012 release.

If you'd like to recommend a great book, share a recipe for homemade cake of any kind or have a tip for getting your children to do what you say the *first* time you say it, Ann would love to hear from you through her website, www.AnnChristopher.com.

Sinful seduction

ANN CHRISTOPHER

KIMANI
ROMANCE

To Richard

Special thanks to my editor, Kelli Martin, for all her
enthusiastic support in bringing The Twins of Sin to life.

KIMANI PRESS™

Recycling programs
for this product may
not exist in your area.

ISBN-13: 978-0-373-86245-0

SINFUL SEDUCTION

www.kimanipress.com

Printed in U.S.A.

Dear Reader,

Allow me to introduce you to Alessandro (Sandro) and Antonios (Tony) Davies, my Twins of Sin. Smart, handsome and fiercely competitive, the two went off to West Point, became army officers and, most recently, fought in Afghanistan.

Only one of them, Sandro, returned.

Imagine Sandro's survivor's guilt. Imagine how much worse it gets when, on a dark and stormy night, Tony's former fiancée shows up on his doorstep, and he discovers that his illicit attraction to her is as strong as ever. Imagine how hard he will fight his feelings, and how hard he will fall for beautiful Skylar.

Most of all—imagine Sandro's stunned disbelief when he discovers…

Well, no. I don't want to ruin it for you!

Happy reading!

Ann

P.S. Please pick up the second book in the series, *Sinful Temptation,* next month!

Chapter 1

This was a mistake, Skylar Lawrence thought, climbing out of her car and staring, with increasing foreboding, at the Sagaponak estate—an English-country type, with shingles and lots of points and dormer windows—sprawled in front of her.

Actually, *mistake* was the wrong word. A mistake was locking your keys in the car and needing AAA to ride to the rescue, or showing up on Tuesday when you and your pal had scheduled lunch for Wednesday. Under a scenario like that, things could turn out well in the end, and if you played it right, you'd have an amusing story to tell the next time you were forced to attend a cocktail party and needed to fill awkward silences with clever chitchat while you nursed your Cosmopolitan.

What she was doing now was courting disaster, plain and simple.

Showing up late at night.

Unannounced.

At the home of her late ex-fiancé's fraternal twin.

But she and Alessandro Davies, a man she'd only met once, nearly two years ago, had unfinished business that couldn't wait any longer.

Not that she was looking forward to it.

Nothing good could come of this, her roiling gut told her, and she usually made it a practice to listen to her gut's communications. Usually. Too bad she couldn't this time and had to race, full speed ahead, toward certain and inevitable disaster. Hell, maybe one of the local news stations should send a satellite truck and a reporter to cover unfolding events. It was sure to be quite the show.

She rang the bell anyway.

Overhead, the sky was doing crazy and alarming things. Intermittent forks of lightning illuminated forbidding and swiftly moving gray clouds that seemed primed to unleash hell any second. Some patches of the sky were navy, while others were the kind of bottomless black that seemed to belong in the farthest reaches of space.

The wind whipped her hair to the left, then to the right, and finally threatened to pick up her whole body and smash it into the nearest mature tree. Only her locked knees kept her from becoming like tumbleweed and blowing away. Somewhere behind the house, unseen but violent, the surf crashed against the shore as though it was determined to eradicate the entire beach by morning.

Shivering inside her jeans now, she wished she'd taken the time to grab a heavier jacket before she had left the city and drove out to the Hamptons, but who expected a near hurricane to hit in the middle of February? If the wind kept up like this, she should probably start worrying about whether the estate had a cellar or not.

Oh, God, though—what if no one was home?

She'd be making like King Lear, raging in the storm, wouldn't she?

She rang the bell again.

It would have made sense to call ahead, of course, but she'd really been counting on the element of surprise—

The door swung open with a creak straight out of a Vincent Price haunted-house movie. She froze, her hand raised midknock, and scrambled to get her senses together.

A man glared up at her from his seat in a wheelchair. His dark hair, buzzed short, was drill-sergeant crisp, as were his white polo shirt and dark trousers. His impressive barrel chest and bulky arms looked as though they belonged to the current heavyweight-boxing champion of the world.

His legs, she realized, were gone below the knee.

Her cheeks flamed as she caught herself staring and looked back at his face.

The flash in his eyes warned that she had exactly one second to state her business and convince him that she meant no harm before he called the police. Actually, no. Something told her that this bulldog wouldn't bother with niceties like consulting the local authorities. He'd probably just pitch her off the nearest cliff and into the surf.

"What the hell?" he demanded in a voice that came from somewhere on the East Coast. "Are you insane, or what?"

"Or what." She cleared her throat, trying to keep her voice strong and unconcerned. "I'm Skylar Lawrence. I'm here to see Alessandro Davies."

"Jesus Christ, lady. It's after eleven o'clock."

"I know. I apologize."

"There's a freaking monsoon out there."

She tried to keep her wind-whipped hair out of her face so she could see. "I'd noticed. Can I come in before I get struck by lightning?"

His lips thinned with apparent indecision, and she sent up a quick prayer that his innate suspicion would give way to what she hoped was the heart of a gentleman. Shooting a glare at the sky, which now looked like the swirling contents of a witch's cauldron, he backed up enough to open the door an additional inch, let her edge inside, and shut the door behind her.

A quick glance up and down the forbidding hallway made her wonder if she should go back outside and take her chances with the elements.

They were in a massive foyer, the centerpiece of which was a staircase that curved up into the invisible depths of the floor which was where they probably kept the bodies.

She couldn't see much else of the house. They either hadn't paid their electric bill or didn't believe in lamps, and she therefore had to rely on the sketchy moonlight streaming in through the windows. But it did seem like they could either go left or right. The left option apparently led to an abyss. To the right was a long stretch of hallway leading to an open door through which a crack of yellow illumination was visible.

Skylar shivered, trying to get a grip on the dread that trickled down her spine like a single drop of ice water. "Is Alessandro home?"

Mr. Friendly folded his Popeye forearms across his chest and put another roadblock in her way. "This ain't a good time, if you know what I'm saying. You might want to come back—"

"No, I don't want to come back." She didn't mean to be rude, but really, did this genius think she'd show up in the middle of the night like this if she had some other option? "I didn't want to drive all the way out here in the first place, but Alessandro forced my hand. So, if you don't mind, just go get him, tell him I'm here, I'll say my piece, and I'll get out of your hair. Okay?"

He was so not moved by her plea. "And what've you got going on that's so doggone important, eh? Someone die or something?"

"Bingo. My ex-fiancé died. Antonios. Alessandro's twin brother. As you surely know already." Even in the relative darkness, she could see the color leach out of his skin, making his pale face stand out like a beacon against the gloom. "Can I see Alessandro now?"

"Mother of Mary," the guy breathed. "I should have recognized you. Tony showed us your picture. You're Sky?"

As always, the use of Tony's nickname for her and, hell, the memory of Tony himself, made her throat seize up. "Skylar, yes."

"He talked about you." The guy swallowed audibly, no doubt trying to wrestle his own memories into submission. "You know he loved you, right?"

There it was: the sharp edge of that same dagger carving up her heart. Again. Always. Blinking back a tear or two—she would not do this, not now—she swiped at her nose and did her best to produce a smile. It didn't work. "Thank you for telling me. Did you serve with Tony?"

"Yeah." At long last, the guy seemed to remember his manners and stuck out a hand to shake hers in his crushing grip. "Yeah. I'm, ah, Michael Bianchi. People call me Mickey. I'm, ah, sorry for your loss."

Her loss.

If there was an appropriate response to that sentiment, she'd never been able to manage it. This time, she didn't even try. A nod would have to do.

Mickey murmured something unintelligible that sounded gruff and sympathetic.

They both shifted uncomfortably.

"Well," he said, "I'd better get the boss for you—"

A sudden bang and the shatter of glass came from

somewhere on the second floor—her first thought was a shutter flying into a window and breaking it—and they heard the ferocious whistle of the wind as it swept down the staircase to meet them. She could just make out the flap of expensive drapes on the other side of the upstairs railing and feel the damp chill of the rain, which was now, apparently, falling in sheets.

"*Shit.* Not the mural. *Not the mural.*" Forgetting all about her for the moment, Mickey wheeled around his chair and raced off to a small elevator for damage control.

Skylar took a couple quick steps after him, because God knew what a few minutes of rain could do to the undoubtedly high-end silk drapes, furniture and gleaming floors in this beachfront palace, and maybe she could help.

But then, lured by the insistent siren call of the light in the other direction, she hesitated.... Stopped.... Turned.... Tried to talk sense into herself and resist the irresistible.

She could wait for Mickey to come back and announce her to Alessandro, but why? Hadn't she waited too long already? Did it matter if she saw Alessandro now or five minutes from now? It wasn't like she could scrape together another ounce of patience anyway.

The decision made, she crept down the hallway to the right.

Another mistake, she knew, but her feet kept walking her toward that yellow glow. Whatever power she may have had to stop and go back was chomped on and swallowed up by the kind of driving curiosity that had always spelled trouble for her, especially where Alessandro Davies was concerned.

He was in that room, her instincts screamed, and tonight, for once, he couldn't hide from her.

She paused at the threshold, her hand on the ornate brass knob, and that was when she heard a low cry that was as painful as any injury she'd ever sustained.

It was the raw, wounded sound of a heart breaking.

A smart woman would have turned and run. Not just away from this door, but out of this house, away from this estate and, just to be safe, off this island. It was foolish to confront a lion in his den, yeah, but she could survive a little foolishness now and then. Cornering a lion in pain was idiotic, if not outright suicidal, and she wasn't ready to check out of life just yet.

And still her feet kept walking, propelled by an irrational but powerful urge to help Alessandro.

Without bothering to knock, she stepped inside the room, just far enough to survey the landscape, get her bearings and, if need be, make a speedy escape.

It was a study of some sort, she saw at a glance. The kind of darkly masculine domain that a nineteenth-century woman would never dream of breaching. She squinted into the gloom, identifying the furniture. There was an overstuffed leather sofa and wingback chairs, draped windows that blocked out even the suggestion of moonlight. An unlit fireplace topped by an ornate mirror, bookshelves crowded with leather-bound volumes and a massive wooden desk that could probably double as a dining-room table capable of seating twenty-five people.

A single corner lamp cast enough light to ensure that she wouldn't bump into anything, but not enough for anything approaching warmth.

Wow. Three seconds inside this room of despair and Skylar almost had depression herself. Nice.

It got worse.

Alessandro Davies was sitting on a bench in front of a full-size grand piano. Its lid was closed and it was covered with a heavy tarp, but he had one edge peeled back to reveal some of the keys. His fingers were poised as if he intended to play something but then, for no apparent reason, he pounded the keyboard, making her jump with the ringing bang of angry notes.

What the—?

Lunging to his feet, he pivoted and crossed the room. In front of the fireplace now, he bowed his head and braced his hands on the mantel, as though it was the only thing keeping him from dropping to the plush rug on the floor. His broad shoulders were stooped, his posture defeated. Though he had his back to her, part of his face was visible in the mirror, and it was a jumble of features twisted into unmistakable anguish.

Her heart contracted as though his pain had seeped into her body.

She didn't have to look far for the source of his turmoil. There was a makeshift shrine on the mantel, the remnants of a fallen soldier's life.

A pair of weathered boots with laces untied.

A pair of white dress gloves.

The metallic gleam of dog tags.

A Bible.

A small but beautiful oil painting of the sun.

Collectively, they added up to the only parts of Tony Davies that had returned from Afghanistan intact.

Seeing all this reminded her, in excruciating detail, of the day she got the news. That a convoy with both twins in it had been hit by an IED as it crossed a bridge. That Sandro had been gravely injured, and Tony's body had been lost, presumably in the swirling river.

That Tony was presumed dead, and the last thing she had ever said to him was that she didn't love him enough to marry him.

Today was their birthday, of course. The Davies twins, Alessandro and Antonios, should both be turning thirty-six today. Except that they'd both gone off to war and one of them had never come back. Tony was gone now, obliterated by a roadside bomb, and that bomb was still doing its damage, wasn't it? The gift of destruction that kept on giving.

Riveted, she watched Alessandro, unable to leave and incapable of going to him and offering comfort. Because what would she say?

That she didn't blame him for merely being wounded

in the explosion that had killed his twin? That she was sorry? Weren't they all?

No. There was nothing she could say.

He reached out, skimming the mementos with his long-fingered hand. His touch was so gentle, so reverent, that she knew she was seeing way too much and should look away from this intimate moment between a remaining brother and his ghosts.

But she didn't. Couldn't.

And then, without warning, his quiet sadness yielded to something edgier and much more troubling. Wheeling around, Alessandro strode to the console against the wall, reached for a crystal decanter and sloshed some liquor into a tumbler, spilling as much as he poured.

A beat's hesitation passed.

Then he leaned his head back and drank so deeply that Skylar could almost feel the burn in her own throat. He swallowed hard. Gasped. Rolled his shoulders a couple of times, clearly trying to decide which path to take. Apparently choosing oblivion, he reached for the decanter again and filled it up.

But this time he paused with the glass halfway to his lips, his attention snagged by a framed photograph on the table nearest the sofa. The light was just good enough for her to see that it was Tony's formal graduation portrait from West Point.

Wearing his dress uniform and the hard stare that soldiers always do when posing for pictures, Tony looked young and proud and, worse, invincible. She had the ridiculous thought that if she could sneak inside that photo and whisper to that young man that he had less than twenty years to live, he would laugh with disbelief and pity at her obvious confusion.

The sight of him was too much for her and, apparently, for Alessandro.

With an angry roar, he raised his arm and lashed out, sending the tumbler crashing into the picture and knocking it to the floor in a spectacular shower of flying glass shards and scotch. Drops of liquor rained down on the furniture for what seemed like forever, and her intrusion, finally, registered with her brain.

She'd seen too much. Gone too far. Stayed too long.

But it was too late.

Alessandro had heard her sharp cry of surprise, or maybe his peripheral vision caught the jerk of her arm as she pressed her hand to her mouth. His head came up and his eyes flashed to the mirror over the mantel, where he finally saw her standing behind him.

Their gazes locked and held.

The intensity of his expression rocked her back on her heels. It was as powerful as the percussion wave from a bomb, and twice as dangerous.

In the mirror, she saw a slow, hard smile pull on one corner of his mouth. Turning, he gave her a mocking little nod that was as insulting as he could make it.

Hating him suddenly, she tried to ignore the way her heartbeat skipped and stuttered when he looked at her, the sudden lack of breathable air in here, and the shivering awareness in her skin.

"Weli, well, well." His deceptively soft voice—deeper than she'd remembered it; more startling—was so heavy with sarcasm that she was surprised the words didn't drop out of the air and clatter to the floor one by one. "If it isn't my brother's beloved ex-fiancée. You're just in time to join the party."

Chapter 2

Now that the moment was here, Skylar was disturbed to discover that her courage had not made the long trip out to the Hamptons with her after all. Without it, her mouth was dry, her knees weak and her resolve sketchy at best.

She felt, in a word, exposed.

That was the problem with Alessandro; he affected her on some core cellular level that defied explanation. His gaze burned her. His energy, which bubbled beneath the surface of that quiet facade, electrified her. Being in his presence felt equally dangerous and exhilarating, and she'd known it would be this way.

Which was probably why she couldn't stay away.

The one time she'd met him, all those months ago, was not enough.

The woman in her (and, face it, she was all woman, wasn't she?) couldn't help wondering what it would be like to get under this man's skin and caught up in his arms. What would he do? Driving curiosity had her in a choke hold, despite her clanging nerves. There was passion somewhere deep inside him, and the right woman could tap into it.

And then...

And then, she suspected, all his outer ice would melt into steam.

It was his eyes, which were every bit as intense as she'd remembered. Those brown eyes could change on a dime, and all his expressions were fascinating. Right now, for instance, he'd already locked away the sadness she'd glimpsed a minute ago, and his brows had flatlined into a piercing and chilly stare that told her there'd be hell to pay for showing up here.

Quiet hell, but still hell, because he'd probably hoped never to see her again. Too bad he wasn't going to get his wish. Not this time.

Riveted by everything about him, her body reacting in secret, feminine ways, she couldn't speak. She could barely breathe.

Alessandro Davies made her blood surge, her belly tighten and her breasts ache.

She stared. He stared back, arrested and utterly still. Neither of them blinked.

The tension swirled around them, binding them together and spiking until, with sudden and absolute clarity, she realized that they were in a battle of wills, she and Sandro. What was the prize? She had no idea. But she never backed away from a challenge.

Never.

He spoke first, deploying that deep rasp against her. "Cat got your tongue? I asked if you wanted to join me."

She gave the mess on the floor a pointed glance. "I think I'll pass. Doesn't look like much of a party. Happy birthday, by the way."

His eyes widened. "You remember that?"

"Could I forget?"

Another of those pregnant moments passed. Along the length of her spine and up into her scalp, she felt nerve endings prickle to life. It was all she could do not to shiver.

"Why don't you call it a night?" she suggested.

His mouth softened a fraction in a precursor to a smile that would probably never come. "I was just getting started."

"Maybe you should stop. I don't think you can handle your liquor."

There it was. Another flash in those shadowed eyes. A sign that she'd…what? Dinged his pride? Irritated him? Infuriated him?

"I see. So you showed up in the middle of the night to criticize me in my own house?"

"No. I came to talk to you, and I was forced to come out here because you've been ignoring my phone calls for weeks." Tired of the oppressive gloom, which wasn't helping her skittering nerves, she marched to the nearest lamp and clicked it on before turning back to gauge his response. Time to put on her big-girl panties and take charge a little. "Why is it so dark in this house? What're you—a vampire?"

"Do feel free to make yourself at home."

She ignored the sarcasm. "And did you forget—it's my house, too, isn't it?"

"Could I forget?" He eased closer with a step that was slow and measured, and yet somehow simultaneously—magically—gave the impression that he couldn't reach her fast enough and planned to tear her limbs from her body when he did. "You reached the pot of gold at the end of your rainbow, didn't you? That's pretty good work for an engagement that only lasted, what, ten minutes."

Ah. There it was. The accusation of moneygrubbing that was the inevitable result of dating a man from a wealthy family when you were the product of a hardworking teacher mom and a preacher dad from Harlem.

The Davies family had, decades ago, parlayed their New York City auction house, Davies & Sons, into a major player in the global art and jewelry market, giving Christie's and Sotheby's a run for their money. Not that she'd cared about any of that when she and Tony had made the disastrous choice to romanticize their friendship.

Sandro was assuming a lot of facts not in evidence.

That she'd never truly cared about Tony.

That she'd callously broken his heart right before his final deployment.

That she was happy to have been mentioned in Tony's will and wanted his wealth.

Sandro believed the worst about her, and it hurt badly enough to leave a mark. It shouldn't, but it did.

It did not, apparently, matter to him that her little family had worked their asses off, getting Skylar through The Masters School, an exclusive New York boarding school just outside the city, or that Skylar had gone on to college and veterinary school at Ohio State and now had a thriving practice in Boston.

No.

Apparently the only thing that mattered out here, in the rarefied air of the Hamptons, was how blue your blood was and how much money daddy had in the bank.

Well, screw Alessandro Davies and his assumptions.

"Why are you so convinced I'm a gold digger?" Firing up, she pointed a finger right at his haughty face. "Why not give me the benefit of the doubt? What did I ever—"

He studied her with cool disdain, the way she imagined he'd look if he accidentally poured sour milk in his morning cereal. "Maybe it was your whirlwind courtship. What did it take? Two months for you to hook up with my brother and get him to pop the question?"

"Wow." She arched a brow. "So I'm Bathsheba now? I had no idea I was so seductive or your brother was so gullible. Thanks for the compliment—"

"And then, what—another two months to kick him to

the curb and send him spiraling out of control when he went back to Afghanistan? You knew this, right? That he was reckless at the end? Hell, he probably jumped on that IED just to get a little relief from the pain you caused him."

Bastard.

Blind fury at this injustice made her head spin.

"Did it ever occur to you that I cared about your brother? Or that I thought I was doing the right thing by breaking up with him?" God, her voice was ragged now; she could barely force it to work, and she hated him for reducing her to this mess. "Or that I never asked him to name me in his will? Did it ever cross your mind that I didn't want to receive his portion of this estate?"

"No." He stared at her, his rigid face so hard and unforgiving it would have been at home next to a bust of Julius Caesar. "It never did."

Her mouth twisted with the effort to hold back a snarl. "Wow. It's amazing to think that a bastard like you could be twins with a—"

"A what? A saint like him?" He shrugged, but the nonchalant gesture didn't quite fit with the sharp glint in his eyes. There was that crack in his facade again, the only hint that she'd ever get to let her know that he was human, after all, and this conversation affected him. "Ah, well. You can't explain genetics, can you?"

Some inner voice—or maybe it was a demon—urged her on, and she decided to go with it. He'd stabbed her in the heart with his accusations, and if there was any way for her to punish him back, she was damn sure going to try.

"You know, I'm wondering. Are you so sure that your brother was only lovable because of his money, or is there something about me in particular that gets under your skin?"

He stiffened, and that was answer enough.

Oh, God.

Turning the lights on, she belatedly realized, had been a mistake. They were toe to toe now, both brimming with agitated aggression, and the flashes of lightning, quickly followed by doomsday booms of thunder, drove up the room's crackling energy into a zone that could optimistically be called dangerous.

He was handsome. Moodily, wickedly and devastatingly handsome. His hooded eyes were soulful and wounded, his nose and cheekbones were harsh slashes of bone, and his lips were curved and full. If someone could splice the best features of Denzel Washington and a young Marlon Brando together, Alessandro Davies would be the unforgettable result.

And the body—don't get her started. He was somewhere just under six feet, she thought, and had the tough and lean lines of the soldier he'd been until that career-ending explosion in Afghanistan, the same one that'd claimed his brother. There was something about the way he carried himself that caught the eye—her eye—and held it. Straight and proud, with wide shoulders, a flat belly and the kind of rounded butt and hard thighs she was more used to seeing on NFL running backs. He was a man's man who did not, she was sure, take any shit from anyone. Ever.

Now that she'd turned on that cursed lamp, she could see all of him, up close and in the kind of high-def detail that emphasized the dark beginnings of tomorrow's beard under that brown skin. Now that he was this near, she could smell the liquor on his breath and, worse, the sophisticated scent of him, something with spices and leather. Now that their wills were locked in battle, she felt the slow curl of heat deep in her belly.

Her former fiancé, Tony, was Sandro's twin, yeah, but they'd been fraternal all the way. Tony had possessed none of these arresting features or qualities, or, if he did, they weren't arranged anything like *this*.

The genetics of it didn't make sense; he was right about that.

"What do you want?" There was a ruthless new quality in his low voice now, a take-no-prisoners finality that told her he wanted her gone and would do whatever it took to make that happen. "You want me to cut you a check with a lot of zeros so I can buy your share of the estate I grew up on? Is that it? Tony's been dead too long for you to just be discovering you're pregnant or any nonsense like that—or were you here to announce that you've had a secret love child and think you're entitled to support? Help me out here."

She flinched, her head full of a frantic buzzing, as though he'd slapped her.

So this was what he thought of her.

Actually, no. His opinion wasn't about her at all, and she was woman enough and self-confident enough to know that. It was all about the unexpected and guilty chemistry they'd shared the night they met, and the darkness bottled up inside his soul. What kind of pain did he carry around every day? What kind of demons dogged his footsteps?

Staring into those cold eyes, she told him the truth.

"If that's what you really think, I feel sorry for you."

He winced and paced away from her, back into the shadows, withdrawing into the cave of his unhappiness and nursing his hurts like a wounded bear.

His silent pain seeped into her bones, and she wished—

Ah, hell. She had no idea what she wished, which was just as well.

He was leaning his elbows on the mantel and had his head in his hands, rubbing his temples with enough force to wipe off his entire face.

Raw emotion propelled her; logical thought never entered into it. Coming up behind him, she rested her hands on his rigid shoulders and squeezed, her aching heart full of apologies.

"Sandro—"

Jerking free, he wheeled around to roar at her with the full might of his fury.

"Don't touch me!"

His rejection rolled over her in a flattening wave, and she staggered back a step, stunned and hurt. The way he glared at her—with all that bottomless venom—hurt. He'd hurt her again. Everything about him hurt her, and she hated him for it.

A vindictive little voice began to whisper inside her head.

She thought about the reason she'd come all the way out here, the lawyer she'd hired, and the executed paperwork in her purse. She thought about how she'd signed back over her unwanted share of the estate to Sandro, its rightful owner, and how she'd planned to do the right thing.

Well, screw that.

Just because she was mature enough to see that this man was in pain didn't mean that she could forgive him for the tiny little knives he kept stabbing in her heart.

It'd be a cold day in hell before she gave the papers to him. If he wanted them, he knew where she lived. He could find her at home in Boston, and then he could do a little begging.

The thought did her a world of good.

"Screw you," she told him.

With that, she grabbed her purse, pivoted and stalked out, back through the saturating darkness the way she'd come, ignoring Alessandro's sharp "Skylar!" as she went.

"What the hell?" Mickey's face appeared over the upstairs railing. "I thought you left!"

She kept going, ignoring him, too. From the corner of her eye she noticed another, slighter, figure in the gloom behind Mickey, but she didn't get a good look.

Was that Alessandro's son, then? Well, God bless him if it was. Tony had told her all about him. He'd also mentioned how the boy's mother had abandoned the family when Sandro got home from his first deployment, and now lived somewhere in California. Poor kid. There was no telling what his life was like with his mother three thousand miles away, his father locked behind a layer of permafrost and this living crypt for a home while he struggled with adolescent hormone poisoning.

Poor kid, she thought again. He didn't have a chance, did he?

Everything about this wretched estate broke her heart, and she couldn't escape fast enough.

Throwing open the heavy front door, she hurried down the steps and into the storm, which had graduated from troublesome to nasty. Icy water assaulted her face and drenched her to the skin as she stumbled across the cobblestone driveway. The frigid rain kept coming with a driving force, as though she'd pulled the chain on a showerhead outside an Arctic igloo.

And it was dark now. Deep-space dark. Pit-of-hell dark.

It was all she could do to stagger to the car, collapse inside and crank the engine.

Over the wind's relentless howl, she heard urgent male voices shouting warnings behind her, but she ignored them. Like she'd let a little storm trap her here at this miserable house.

Better to escape and find somewhere to stay for the night.

Flipping on her headlights and windshield wipers, she fastened her belt, hit the accelerator and sped off down the long drive toward the main road. If she remembered correctly, there'd been a tiny B and B a couple miles—

Twenty or thirty feet ahead of her, she saw a sight straight out of one of those extreme weather shows on the Discovery Channel: the blinding streak of a forked lightning rod hit a patch of trees just to the right of the road.

No.

In one frantic second, she registered the corresponding crack of thunder and the sudden illumination of wind-tossed leaves and a massive overhanging branch.

No, God. God, please—

Screaming for her life, she stomped on the brake.

It was already too late.

Chapter 3

In the space between when he opened his mouth to shout "Nooo!" and when the last of his voice was swallowed up by the wind's fury, the hundred-year-old oak that Sandro had climbed as a boy and loved his entire life reached out to swallow Skylar's car whole.

Which was further proof that horror caught up with him, even when he wasn't at war.

And here he'd thought he'd seen the worst sights the universe had to offer back in Afghanistan: a new widow, collapsing to the cold and muddy ground, screaming for her husband; the remnants of a suicide bomber who had, seconds before, been a teenage kid without enough fuzz to justify a shave; a blood-matted dog crawling by the side of the road, whining for help that would never come.

Yeah, that was bad.

This was worse.

He'd opened his mouth and spewed venom and his actions had led to reckless behavior. Thanks to him, someone was hurt, possibly dead.

But not beautiful Skylar, God. Not her.

He sprinted flat-out, propelled by the endless blare of her horn and the unmistakable pop of her air bag, his arms and legs pumping so hard he could almost feel the sinew ripping from the bone.

And then he was there, at the car, only he couldn't get anywhere near it because that freaking tree had her caught in its lush green clutches and didn't look like it'd let her go without the threat of a chainsaw.

"Skylar!" he shouted, desperate to see her through the leaves and the water sluicing down the driver's side window. There was no breath in his lungs and his throat seemed to have tightened down to the size of a needle, but her name kept pouring out of him. "Skylar!"

He dove in through the branches, oblivious to their clawing scrapes as they sliced through his skin. There was a ripping sound—his shirt, maybe—and then the searing heat of something trickling down his side and arm mixed with the cold rain. A final lunge and he had the handle in his hand. A flick of his wrist and the dented door was giving way with a resistant squeal, revealing, among other things, a mess of car innards that obscured her lower body.

"Skylar!"

A moan answered him.

She was alive.

A shudder of relief loosened some of the strain through his shoulders, and he was able to think more clearly. Okay, soldier. Assess the situation.

She was leaning back against the headrest, soaking wet, panting and shaking, either with shock or cold. A trickle of blood ran down one temple. As she struggled against the air bag and turned her head to look at him, her eyes were glazed but she'd had the sense to put on her seat belt before she did her bat-out-of-hell routine.

"Jesus." He looked her up and down in a grim search for more serious injuries. "Are you okay?"

Her mouth worked, trying to form words around her chattering teeth. She seemed to be having trouble breathing. "I th-think so."

"Let's get you out of here."

He reached for the seat belt, which was lashed so tight across her body it was a wonder she hadn't been sliced on the diagonal.

If he could just—

That lush mouth of hers firmed into a mulish line and she batted his hands away. "I'm n-not going anywhere with *you*."

Yeah, okay. He deserved that and more. But still—

"You can't stay here."

"T-try me."

He stared at her, studying the fine arch of her brows, the perky tip of her nose, the prominent apples of her cheeks, the dimple on the right side of that mouth and the quiet strength and pride.

She was something, all right. Really something.

But of course he'd known that since he first laid eyes on her.

He opened his mouth, a million *I'm sorry's* and *Please forgive me's* on the tip of his tongue, and all of them trapped, as usual, behind that wall he could never climb.

"I'm—" he began.

"A b-bastard?" she supplied. "A mean SOB? A jack-ass?"

"All of that." His voice was hoarse with shame. "More."

"I'm not a bad person."

"I know."

He really did know. No one could see her wounded pride and dignity in the face of fire and think other-wise. And those accusations he'd thrown at her back in the house? Defense mechanisms, pure and simple, all designed to get rid of her as soon as possible. Because it was dishonorable to look at the woman his dead brother had wanted to marry and wonder what her mouth tasted like and how loud and hot he could get her if he pressed his tongue to the sweet spot between her thighs.

He'd never been a dishonorable man. He wasn't going to start now.

"I'm sorry, Skylar."

"A-are you?"

"Yes."

"Good." She shivered again, reminding him that he needed to get her inside and warm, needed to have a doctor check her for injuries. "D-do you think you could get me out of here?"

"Yeah." Reaching for her, he took her smaller hand in his, marveling at its softness and strength. Touching his dead brother's ex-fiancée felt good. Really good. Too good. "I can do that."

"Call 9-1-1," he yelled at the already soaked Mickey, who was maintaining his vigil atop the front steps.

Mickey waved to let him know he'd heard, then disappeared back into the house.

Now Sandro had a choice to make at this crucial juncture.

Follow the basic rule of trauma injuries and leave her where she was until official help came, or try to get her out himself.

Taking a quick glance around at the holy hell unleashed all around him, he decided that they could call for help all they wanted to, but that didn't mean it'd get there anytime soon.

Since she didn't seem to have any spinal injuries, he decided he'd get her out himself. And while he was doing that, he'd pray that he wasn't exacerbating any hidden but dire internal injuries she may have.

Great. He had a plan.

Only the damn car didn't want to let her go, or maybe the killer tree was to blame. All Sandro knew was that what had formerly been the dashboard was now crushed and pressed down around Skylar's lap, refusing to budge, and the more he couldn't free her, the more panicked he became.

Since it wouldn't do her any good if he hyperventilated and passed out, he worked hard to look upbeat and unconcerned even though his heart was now chugging at a thousand beats per minute.

"Can you lean this way for me, Skylar? I'm going to reach under your arms and try to pull you out, okay? Skylar? Do you hear me?"

Still panting and shivering—actually, the shivering had now progressed to shaking, which was another reason for him to freak the hell out—she tipped up her head to look at him. The glazed layer was thicker over her eyes now, as though shock was trying to lure her away from him and into some abyss.

"*Skylar,*" he barked, fighting the growing terror. "Focus. Stay with me."

"I'm… I'm with you."

She claimed she was with him, yeah, but her voice was other-side-of-the-crypt weak, and that was not reassuring.

"Lift your arms for me. Lean toward me. Can you do that?"

She tried, twisting at the waist and raising her arms with slow effort, as though each one weighed fifty pounds.

That was the best she could do, apparently.

She couldn't free herself and couldn't help him any more than that.

He didn't have to be a medical genius to know that his time was running out. The ongoing lightning strikes illuminated her face enough for him to see that it was dull and colorless. This, in turn, opened up a whole new universe of fear. What about that possibility of a serious head injury? What the hell would he do then?

Hesitating, he weighed his options one more time. A quick glance at the sky revealed a swirling vortex that, with his luck, signaled the apocalypse, and a second glance at the monster tree across the road confirmed the worst. They weren't getting out of here tonight and, unless the Navy sailed a cruiser up the coast right off the house and deployed a SEAL team to come ashore, no one was getting in to provide any medical treatment, either. Not tonight, anyway, and maybe not for days.

It was up to him.

Trying to be as gentle as possible, he put his hands under her arms and eased her…slowly…slowly…around and toward him, pulling her until her back was to his front and he could lock his arms around her chest and get more leverage. She squirmed a little, as though she wanted to help, but her head lolled and she was mostly deadweight.

Still, this was progress, and her upper body was pretty much clear.

"You okay?" he asked in her ear.

She stirred. "N-never…better."

That cut through his fear just enough to make him grin. He had a tough one here. Pressing his face to her cheek—there was still some warmth to her flesh, thank goodness—he gave her a quick kiss, for luck.

"You're awfully brave, ma'am. You sure you're not a soldier?"

"J-just get me out of here."

"Hold on."

Planting his feet wide, trying to get some traction, he pulled. To his grateful astonishment, he felt the slide of her body, inch by slow inch, and he took one step back... another...and her hips and thighs were off the seat and out of the car and she was almost free—

She shrieked, letting loose the kind of high-pitched yell of pain he hadn't heard since he had left the hell-hole that was Afghanistan. Cursing himself, he eased up, ready to put her back on the seat and go at this another way, when she surprised him.

Twisting just enough at the waist, she wriggled and—

That was it. She was free.

He staggered, adjusting to her full weight. A shout of triumph rose to his lips and died a swift death when he saw her lower legs.

Oh, no.

Right leg? Kicking and scrambling for purchase on the cobblestones, trying to get her upright on her own steam.

Left leg? Stiff and lifeless, a mess of torn jeans and dark wet that could only be blood.

"You're hurt, Sky," he told her, shifting his grip to her waist and helping her put her arm around his neck.

"Really?" she breathed, her face twisted against the pelting rain and the pain. "That must explain the blinding agony in my leg."

The sarcasm told him she was still coherent, which in turn told him that she might not have hit her head that hard, but this was no time for jokes. Who knew how much blood she'd lost already? He had to get her inside.

"I'll carry you."

"I can manage."

"Stubborn, much?"

Opening her eyes, she managed a steely glare.

"Fine," he snapped, tightening his grip on her waist and jerking his head in the direction of the house, which now seemed to be a good three miles away, if not farther. "Be my guest."

Because he knew her dignity demanded it, he held on and kept his mouth shut while she let her bad leg drag and tried to hobble on the good leg. Hell, he even let her try another step, just to show how evolved he was. But on the third hopping lurch, she cried out again, a sharp yelp of pain that felt like it'd been ripped from his own soul, and that was when he hit his limit.

Enough was enough.

Without comment, he swung her off her feet and into his arms as easily as he could, which wasn't easy enough. But at least they were moving now and he wouldn't have to make any more abrupt movements.

She moaned, her head dropping back over the crook in his elbow, but her hand went behind his neck and she held on tight.

"See?" she croaked. "I told you I could do it."

"You showed me."

He hurried as fast as he dared, only his fear of slipping on the wet cobblestones keeping him from breaking into a run. Luckily, she wasn't that heavy, or maybe his adrenaline had kicked so far into overdrive that it didn't matter how heavy she was.

With the way he felt right now? He could lift the tail end of a 747 if that was what it took to get Skylar free.

He took the shallow front steps two at a time and banged through the door and into the foyer, where Mickey, who'd been watching anxiously, was waiting for him.

"Nice save, boss."

"She ain't saved yet, man." Sandro headed down the hall toward the study with Mickey hot on his heels, arms pumping the wheels of his chair. They were halfway there before it dawned on him that he couldn't see a damn thing. "What'd you do to the lights?"

"Tree took the power out," Mickey said.

"That tree wasn't messing around," Sandro muttered.

"You got that right," Skylar said.

"And the mural's ruined. A window broke and the rain's splattering it right now," Mickey added.

Sandro never broke stride. "We've got bigger problems

to deal with right now than losing my mother's Greek mural."

"Greek?" Skylar tried to focus on something other than the pain searing through her.

"She was a Greek scholar," Sandro said. "Hence, the names."

"Good to know." She sagged into him, her strength exhausted and her head lolling.

"Uh, oh," Sandro muttered. "Hurry, Mick."

Mickey sped ahead, lighting the way with a couple of super-bright, battery-operated lanterns that he'd found somewhere, and arrived in the study first. Sliding the coffee table out of the way, he arranged a couple pillows and made room for Sandro to lay Skylar across the leather sofa.

Moving with the care of someone diffusing a roadside bomb near an orphanage, Sandro lowered her, fully willing to die before he caused her any more pain. At last she was settled. He let her go and she dropped her arms, collapsing with palpable relief.

Her eyes closed and she didn't move, although her chest continued to heave with effort, and he wondered again about internal injuries.

That was when his training kicked in. It was showing up pretty late today, all things considered, but better late than never. He was no stranger to crises, and he could handle this one.

Even if he was dripping with clammy sweat despite the frigid rain.

Turning away from Skylar's face, which was contorting again with pain, he confronted Mickey.

"Digital phone went out with the power, right?"

"Yeah," Mickey said. "And my piece-of-shit cell's got no signal."

This was bad news. They wouldn't be calling any medical help lines to speak to a nurse tonight, would they? Still, Sandro had expected as much, so he just nodded.

"I figured." He flashed Mickey a grim smile. "You don't have any training in triage, do you?"

One corner of Mickey's mouth hitched up, and he snorted. "Not me. I faint at the sight of blood. Why don't I just call for a corpsman? That's what they do in all the old war movies."

"I knew I could count on you in a tough spot."

"What can I do you for?"

"I'm going to need the first-aid kit and that bottle of Percocet in my medicine cabinet—"

Skylar stirred, frowning. "I'm not taking that."

Unbelievable. Sandro glowered down at her. "You'll take it."

Those eyes of hers blinked open, a flare of brown fire. "I don't need it."

"You'll need it when I have to cut off your jeans and see what that leg looks like."

"You're not cutting my jeans off—"

He turned back to Mickey, ignoring the rest of her protest. "Get some blankets, too, and, hell, an extra belt or something. We may need to make a tourniquet. Scissors. Maybe some ice for her head. And the scotch. We'll need plenty of scotch—"

"You want me to drink scotch with Percocet?" Skylar asked.

"The scotch is for us. How else are we going to get through the night dealing with you? That's it for now, Mick. Thanks."

"You got it. And here's a blanket to get you started." Mickey tossed over a soft throw from one of the armchairs, left one of the lanterns on the coffee table, and rolled out of the room at top speed, disappearing into the darkness.

Sandro stared down at the patient, who stared back up at him, looking sulky and wary. "What?" she demanded.

Sandro felt his mouth curl with unwilling amusement. "You need to check your attitude. I outweigh you by about a hundred pounds, in case you didn't notice." He paused to give her time to argue, but she didn't. "Right. I want to check your abdomen for internal injuries. I want to make sure that seat belt didn't do any damage."

"I'm fine. And you've got no medical training."

"I've got enough medical training to see if your belly's swollen."

"It's not. And we're stuck here anyway, so what would—"

"I'd go for help, that's what."

This prospect seemed to take some of the vinegar out of her. She gasped. "It's not safe out there—"

"I know it's not safe, which is why I'm not thrilled about going back out in the storm, but I'm happy to do it if the seat belt sliced your liver in half. So why don't you let me check your belly and we can move on to bickering about another one of your body parts?"

"Fine." Closing her eyes again, she jerked up the bottom of her coat and peeled back her shirt, revealing a wide swath of smooth flesh between the bottom of her black—black!—bra and the top of her low-riding jeans. "Hurry. I'm tired."

Riveted by the sight of that caramel skin, Sandro experienced a flash of temporary paralysis. This was an emergency, true, but he'd have to be dead and cremated, with his ashes scattered to the four winds, not to notice the curve of waist as it flared to her hips, or the tautness of her abdomen, or the dip of her belly button, which, let's face it, would be a fine place for a man's tongue to explore.

Blinking, he recovered quickly and sat at her hip, facing her.

Right. Check for swelling, Davies.

Pressing firmly in what he hoped was a reasonable version of palpating, he made his systematic way from one side to the other, checking for sore or swollen spots and trying to ignore the sweet softness of her warm flesh.

"Here?" he murmured.

She shook her head.

"How about here?"

Another head shake.

"How about your ribs? You've got a nasty bruise here—"

"Ow!"

"Sorry. It doesn't feel swollen, though. I think we can rule out internal injuries."

She nodded.

Good. Great. Wonderful.

There being no further reason to touch her right now, he withdrew his hands and expelled a breath. For reasons that he didn't care to explore, he felt a little shaky, but this was not the time to flake out, not when her temple was still oozing from a jagged cut that looked about two inches long.

"Okay. Let's check your head—"

Those eyes blinked open, looking brighter. Too bright. "I'm cold."

He could tell. If she kept up with the shivering, the whole sofa would be shaking soon. "Let's get you out of this wet coat."

Cooperative for once, she rose up just enough for him to ease the soggy gray wool down her arms and off. She was about to collapse back against the pillows, but they weren't done yet.

"You need to take everything off, Skylar."

"D-don't even try it."

Perfect. Her teeth were chattering again, she was probably in shock or heading for shock, and she thought he was a pervert. Hell, maybe she was right. Though he intended to be gentlemanly about it and look away at any crucial moments, he'd hardly run screaming from the room if he accidentally caught a glimpse of, say, her breasts.

But she was injured and they didn't have time for this yammering debate.

"Think, Sky. I can't get you warm if your clothes are soaked."

"I don't—"

"Look," he said flatly. "You can do it, or I'll do it. Your choice."

Her cheeks burned red hot. "I should never have come here."

"No," he agreed, arranging the blanket over her upper body and arms to preserve any remnants of her modesty. A muscle began to tick in the back of his jaw, and there wasn't a freaking thing he could do about it. Already he was contemplating the moment when Skylar left, leaving him in the darkness again, and the loss tasted bitter. Which was ridiculous, because it wasn't like she was his to lose. "You shouldn't have come."

Staring at the outline of her arms beneath the blanket, trying to make sure she took the damn shirt off while simultaneously trying not to think about what she was revealing, he waited, giving her time for something he knew she'd never accomplish.

Sure enough.

She fumbled, taking forever with the top button, and there was no way she'd ever manage to undo one button, much less a row of them. Her fingers were way too cold and clumsy.

"Need help?" he asked softly.

Her expression murderous, she gave a sharp nod.

Ignoring the growing hum of his blood as it coursed through his veins, Sandro reached for the blanket so he could get her out of those clothes.

Chapter 4

Skylar wasn't sure which was worse: the searing pain in her leg or the galling humiliation of being dependent upon Sandro Davies, a man who clearly didn't want to be bothered with her and was probably regretting his decision not to let the killer tree keep her.

Then she risked another glance up at Sandro's hard features and decided that, yeah, the humiliation was much worse. The pain, after all, would eventually go away.

How on God's green earth had she gotten herself into this fix? It was all her fault for running out into the rain and driving off like a maniac. Well, no. Her fault went way beyond that. It was all her fault for coming out here to this storm-swept fortress of solitude to confront

Sandro when it would have been easier to just mail him the paperwork handing over her half of the estate.

And, of course, it was her fault for not being able to forget his face and the time they'd met. Clearly, she hadn't put her mind to it and tried hard enough.

Now she was paying the price. Served her right.

Hadn't she known, the second that she knocked on the door, that this night was destined for disaster? Well, here it was. Disaster in the form of the brooding sexy man who hated her.

God, her head was spinning.

If things kept up like this, she'd be barfing on him soon, and wouldn't that be an appropriate finish to this lovely trip to the Hamptons?

She winced and closed her eyes again, trying to will away the pain, the bone-freezing cold and the embarrassment. Unfortunately, the facial gesture sent a flash of pain pulsing from her temple through the top of her head. For added kicks, she felt the warm trickle of blood, as though the wound hadn't quit oozing yet. Wonderful. With a weak moan, she reached for the spot with shaky fingers, meaning to do something with it, maybe press or rub the cut into submission. Sandro forced something soft (a handkerchief?) into her hand.

"Use this."

His hand on top of hers, he guided the cloth into position and pressed down. It hurt. A lot. This, in turn, kicked off another wave of nausea and, to her further shame, the hot sting of tears that insisted on leaking out the corners of her eyes.

"You're not crying, are you?" he murmured.

If there was any sort of a god at all, he/she/it would punish this bastard—severely and repeatedly—for taunting her in her moment of weakness.

Taking a shuddering breath, she pulled it together. "No," she snapped. "I never cry."

"Good. Let's work on your clothes before you get hypothermia."

Without further ado, he reached under the bottom of the blanket and started on the top button of her shirt, which he undid with a brisk efficiency that made her wonder how often he undressed women without looking. Ha. Dumb question. The rest of the buttons followed, and soon he was pulling the edges of her shirt apart.

She could feel the fluffy tickle of the soft blanket brushing against her skin, but his fingers never touched her flesh. Was he avoiding that contact?

And why, with everything else going on, was she hungry for it?

Things went smoothly until it was time for him to ease the shirt past her shoulders and down her arms, when he hesitated.

Some devil made her open her eyes.

To her keen shock, he was staring at her, and their gazes connected with a jolt. A trick of the light put half his face in shadow, hardening his features until his straight nose was a knife's blade and his high cheekbones might have been sculpted from marble. His lips had thinned, creating the threat of cruelty, but a mouth that lush could never be anything other than sensual.

His expression was intense but otherwise unreadable and impenetrable. What made him so intent? Anger? Fear? Frustration? Who the hell knew? She'd have better luck catching the next flight to Egypt and trying to get a bead on the Sphinx's mood.

She stilled, her pain forgotten.

He cleared his throat, looking away. "Sit up for me."

She did. Well, she tried. But the slight change in elevation set off another ripple of wooziness, and the whole exercise quickly turned into more than she could handle. But before she could slump back against the pillows, Sandro went to work. One of his strong hands slid around to the small of her back, keeping her in a seated position and soothing as it went, and held her steady while the other hand ran across the bare skin of her shoulders, easing the shirt down one arm, then the other.

With the wet cold gone, all she could feel was the heat of his fingers. They felt like heaven, spreading warmth, energy and strength in a radius that went far beyond the point of contact. She almost cooed with stolen pleasure.

Was this why she'd wanted him to touch her? Why she'd needed it?

A twinge in her ribs snapped her out of it. "Ow," she complained.

"What?"

"My ribs."

He nodded, focusing on her clothes, and she tried to get a grip.

What was she doing? What had gotten into her? Heat spread across her cheeks—well, at least she wasn't quite so cold any more, so that was progress, eh?—and, with her free hand, she clutched the blanket to her chest, making sure it didn't slip.

It was all the protection she had, and they were close enough to kiss.

Focus, Sky, she told herself sternly.

She opened her mouth, with something about keeping her underwear on hovering on the tip of her tongue, but his hands were already on the move again. They slid to the center of her back and met at the clasp of her bra. One flick of his wrists and the thing came loose, and then the straps were falling over her shoulders, just begging to be tugged off.

Keeping his lids lowered, he obliged. She flowed with him, turning from side to side to get her arms free—

"Hey! Whoa! What's going on in here?"

Mickey was back, but Skylar couldn't take her eyes off Sandro's intriguing face. There was the quick flash of his eyes, the infinitesimal tightening of his jaw, and then he was easing her onto the pillows and moving back into his own space farther down on the sofa. He took a minute to adjust the blanket over her torso again, and then he was back to business.

"You're just in time," he told Mickey, who was hovering in the doorway with a bunch of stuff on his lap. "You got those scissors?"

Mickey couldn't seem to get his jaw off the floor. "I, ah…yeah. I got 'em right here. I got everything."

Sandro stared at him, one eyebrow heading north with growing impatience. "Were you planning to hand them over?"

"Sure." Mickey wheeled all the way into the room. "Here you go."

"Great. Thanks." Sandro rose and strode over to help Mickey put the stuff on the table. "And could you get us some ice? For her head."

"Yeah. Sure." Mickey wheeled around for the door again, but not before hesitating and shooting Skylar a look that was long, curious and speculative. "You got it."

Skylar hitched the blanket higher, up to her chin.

Sandro, tracking Mickey's line of sight, frowned.

"Now would be good," he said sharply.

Mickey swung back around to Sandro, looking amused now, judging by the wry curl of his mouth. "Happy to get out of your way anytime you want, boss," he said. "Just ask."

He rolled out, disappearing into the darkness again, and Skylar could swear she heard a chuckle echo down the hall. When he was gone, she had to work hard to look in Sandro's direction.

He didn't seem too anxious to meet her gaze, either.

Turning away from her, he reached behind his neck and, in one swift movement, yanked off his sweatshirt along with the T-shirt over his head. The next thing she knew, she was confronted with gleaming brown skin and the toned and rippled physique of a man who'd received at least twice his share of beautiful genes when God was divvying out the world's supply of attractive.

There went all of the air, sucked right out of the room. "What are you doing?" she cried.

"Here." With jerky movements that only underscored the flex and play of those glorious muscles, he tossed the T-shirt, which had managed to stay dry under the bulky sweatshirt, to her. "Do us all a favor and put this on."

Fumbling—it wasn't every day that she witnessed God's creative brilliance in full force and effect quite like *that*—she managed to catch it before it whacked her across the face. But then another distraction arose.

In the half second before Sandro stood and pulled the sweatshirt back on, she glimpsed a horrific scar, raised, puckered and glaring across the smoothness of his skin, extending from the middle of his back, down through that perfect six-pack and disappearing south of his waistband in front.

Skylar gasped, surprise and concern making her nosier than she'd normally be. "My God. What happened to—"

But Sandro had already stalked off, disappearing into the shadowy edges of the room beyond the lamp's glow, and she heard the clink of a glass and the splash of liquid. Then he was back, passing her a Big Gulp portion of scotch in a crystal tumbler and keeping one for himself.

"Stop yakking and drink up. You need it. Cheers."

With that, he tossed back his scotch, reached for a lethal pair of scissors that looked like they doubled as hedge trimmers and eyed her leg.

Whoa. Skylar's head swam again, this time with the surplus of things happening that she needed to stop. ASAP.

"Don't come near me with those scissors—"

His brows flattened.

"And forget about the scotch. I'm not drinking it."

No way, Jose. The last thing she needed right now was to ingest something that would make her loopier and lower her resistance to…she didn't even want to think about it. Not that she thought Sandro or Mickey would take advantage of her; she'd stake her life that they were honorable men who wouldn't dream of hurting a woman. It was just that her thoughts and feelings veered off in unsettling directions where Sandro was involved, especially when he touched her.

That implacable and unblinking gaze of his nailed her between the eyes and held until some of her defiance melted away and she began to squirm. Then she began to feel foolish, which pissed her off. How could she win here? Matching wits with him was like being in a staring contest with an eagle.

"I'm trying to take care of you," he quietly reminded her. "Do you understand that? Do you even know why you're disagreeing with me, or is it just a reflex?"

That did it. Now officially feeling like an idiot, she looked away, raised the glass, and drank.

The effect was immediate. Fire sizzled down her throat like a lit fuse, hit her belly and made a shock wave of heat pulse through her body. She coughed… wheezed…and drank again, draining the glass, which she thunked on the coffee table.

Buzzing pleasantly, she glared at Sandro, who was giving her that quirked-brow look of cool amusement.

"Happy?" she demanded.

"I'm delirious with glee."

The liquor quickly took over (at least that's what she'd tell herself in the morning), lowering her inhibitions and making her recklessly embrace her desire to rattle his cage.

Thus, she dropped the front of the throw, flashing her breasts at him as she threaded her arms through the T-shirt and yanked it down over her head.

Her reward? The sharp hitch of his breath.

Leaning back against the pillows, she risked a quick glance at his openmouthed face. He looked stunned, much to her immense satisfaction. Most likely he was dismayed that someone with such negligible cleavage had the nerve to flash anyone, but still. The reprieve from his nonstop commands felt good. For a millisecond.

Then the intimacy of his still-warm shirt against her bare breasts hit her in a rush, bringing her far too close to him. Her head was a constant throb of pain and her leg screamed, but she could still smell the clean musk of him, and the subtle scent of leather wrapped in something spicier and more exotic.

It was almost like being folded into his arms, and that was something she didn't need to be thinking about. So she focused on overcoming the immediate crisis, which was about to get much worse, pain wise.

"Let's go," she barked.

Sandro blinked and snapped back to attention. Resuming his position on the sofa at her hip, he gently inserted the scissors' tip beneath the waistband of both her panties and jeans and began to cut along the seam. His expression was grim, his focus absolute. So careful was each snip that she never felt the cold steel of the blades, not even once.

At last he came to the bottom, exposing her bleeding calf. He stared down at it, his jaw tightening, and then reached for one of the washcloths and rubbing alcohol that Mickey had provided.

His gaze flickered up, down the length of her body to her face.

Whatever he'd seen—it wasn't good.

"This will hurt," he warned, placing a towel beneath her leg. "I need to really clean it. We don't know how long you'll be stuck here, and I don't want to take any risks with infection—"

"Just do it," she muttered wearily, closing her eyes and covering them with her arm. "Get it over with."

Foolish words. He poured alcohol over the wound and she jackknifed up with a sharp yell of pain. If he'd used a sword to sever her leg below the knee, it couldn't hurt worse than this.

Somehow, she choked the agony back, locking it away.

In that horrible moment, when she wanted to scream and sob with agony, she remembered Tony, Sandro and all the other soldiers who'd fought overseas, endured true hardships and been injured or killed.

This, on the other hand, was nothing, and she would not cry like a five-year-old.

So she gritted her teeth, gasping for breath.

"I'm sorry," Sandro murmured, over and over again, sounding choked and distraught, and his emotion totally at odds with the cold-eyed raptor's gaze he'd unleashed on her a minute ago. "I don't want to hurt you. I'm sorry, Sky. I'm sorry—"

Sweating now, clammy, she clenched her muscles against the pain and tried not to vomit. She also resisted the urge to check the injury herself and see how much her leg now resembled a lamb shank. Thank God she couldn't see it. That would probably put her right over the edge.

Still, she needed to know. "How bad is it? Don't lie."

"You need stitches. A lot of them."

"But how—"

"Mickey was a medic. A very good medic."

Well, thank goodness for small favors. There was no anesthetic available, no sterile hospital or qualified surgeon to make sure she didn't end up with a Frankenstein scar, but at least Mickey knew how to stitch a wound.

"Get him in here." Her chest heaved, straining against the twin efforts of talking and managing the pain. "And get me some more scotch."

Chapter 5

The lightning and thunder eventually moved on, but the driving rain stayed behind, lashing against the windows in an endless pinging rattle. Skylar fell into a restless and exhausted doze, her stitched-and-bandaged leg now propped on pillows. There'd been some discussion of carrying her upstairs, to one of the bedrooms, but Sandro and Mickey decided it was best not to move her again so soon. So she stayed put on the leather sofa, zoned out on liquor and lost in the dull throb of her injured body and the warmth of the down blankets until a noise woke her.

She stirred and turned her head on the pillow, opening her eyes and then squinting them against the sudden flare of light. Her pupils adjusted, allowing the large form of Sandro to come into view.

He was across the room, where he'd started a fire in the fireplace, which was large enough to park a VW Beetle inside. Wood was piled high, crackling and spitting sparks, and the flickering orange glow illuminated the strain in his tight face as he bent to jab at the logs with a poker.

His head rose, turning in her direction at this sign of life even though she didn't think she'd made a sound. His brow was lined with worry, his voice soft and anxious.

"How are you?"

"'m okay." She tried to speak clearly with her rusty voice, and also tried to give him a reassuring smile, but it was a no-go on both. Her poor brain was too fuzzy to manage any higher functions. "You should go...to bed."

"Nah."

"You need rest." Man, she couldn't even keep her eyes open.

"You need to stop talking and go back to sleep."

Yeah, he was right about that. Her lids drifted shut, but not before she told him what was on her mind.

"Thank you...for taking care of...me," she murmured, fighting the exhaustion. "Sorry I'm such a...pain in the ass."

And then she was asleep again, or thought she was asleep again, except that the low murmur of his voice cut through the fog.

Or was she dreaming?

"You could never be a pain in the ass, beautiful Sky."

* * *

Skylar cried out against a particularly nasty throb in her calf, waking herself with a start. The fire was still blazing, filling the room with heat and the comforting smell of hickory, but she was alone with only the pain and the darkness, which seemed to be edging closer.

A sudden flare of panic made her lever herself up on her elbows, looking for—

"Sandro!"

"I'm here."

A shadow moved, detaching itself from the nearest armchair, and then Sandro *was* there, sitting at her hip again and studying her with anxious eyes. One of his cool hands went to her forehead, probably checking for a fever, and it felt good. Reassuring. That hand was just what she needed, and she didn't want to lose it, so she grasped it by the wrist, holding tight.

"What can I get you, Sky? What do you need?"

The pain, exhaustion and lingering scotch buzz all conspired to make her honest. "I need you to sit with me for a while."

He didn't answer. Maybe he'd been hoping she'd ask for something easy, like a sip of water, then go back to sleep and leave him alone.

His silence shouldn't matter. It didn't matter, she told herself vaguely, succumbing again to the oblivion that kept reaching up, grabbing her by the ankles and pulling her under. Except that it did matter, even on this dark and stormy night when she was stranded and injured, and managing the pain should have been the only thing on her mind.

And the embarrassing confessions just kept coming.

"It makes me so sad," she said as her heavy lids slid lower.

He leaned closer, his thumb now stroking the hair at her uninjured temple, soothing her. "What does, Sky?"

"That you don't like me. I wish...you liked me."

He stiffened, withdrawing his hand and its comfort, which was, she supposed, her punishment for babbling. The last thing she saw before she fell asleep again was the flash of his gaze, which was dark and unreadable, and the flare of his nostrils as he turned his face away from her.

The next time Skylar woke, it was to the weak suggestion of a yellow dawn breaking on the other side of the closed plantation shutters. Was it morning, finally? And she'd lived through the night? And the storm had finally blown itself out?

Glory hallelujah.

She was still wiped out, though. Beyond exhaustion. She wouldn't be hitting the road back to Boston today, that was for sure. Possibly not for several days.

Testing out her leg seemed like a good idea, so she decided to start small, with a toe wriggle. Ouch. Sore—very sore—but not unbearable. So that was progress. What about her side? She shifted against the pillows, twisting at the waist.

Again...ouch. But manageable.

Her bandaged temple was now down to a dull thud, nothing that an extra-strength dose of acetaminophen couldn't handle. And her body temperature felt fine. Neither too hot, nor too cold, so she prayed that Sandro's liberal use of rubbing alcohol last night (the memory made her wince) had done the trick and protected her against infection.

She was, in short, on the road to recovery.

The rhythmic swish of a broom sweeping up broken glass came from the corner, and she raised her head (another *ouch*) to see Sandro dumping the last of the fragments from the smashed photo of Tony, along with the tumbler that had done the smashing, into a trash can. But he kept the picture, shaking off glass dust and placing it, with loving care, on the mantel.

He stared up at it for a minute, lost in his thoughts, and then, apparently feeling the weight of her stare, turned.

If she'd had a rough night, his was not much better, judging from the smudged hollows under his eyes. His face was lined with exhaustion, his jaw prickly with the new day's beard.

He looked absolutely terrible.

That didn't stop his mouth from curling at the edges when he saw that she was awake. The sight of that almost-smile made her skin tingle with awareness, despite her many maladies, and she was glad he didn't unleash the full smile because, in her weakened state, it would probably kill her.

"She lives," he said.

"She lives."

"Did you get any rest?"

"More than you did."

"I wasn't attacked by a tree."

"True."

Her gaze flickered back to the picture of Tony. He seemed to be watching her, possibly accusing her with that hard soldier's stare of his, and it made her uncomfortable enough to look away.

Sandro, naturally, noticed. "You miss him."

It wasn't a question, which was good because she didn't have an answer. "You're angry with him. Probably because he died. Am I right?"

Sandro stilled. It seemed to be a habit of his—being still. She was starting to think of these pregnant pauses as a mechanism he used to wrestle his emotions back under control and get them on lockdown.

To her surprise, he opened the door a tiny crack, letting her see inside for once.

"You're assuming I only have one reason to be angry at my brother."

She hesitated and then decided to press her luck. He wouldn't hit an invalid, surely. "Are you going to tell me?"

"No."

Deflated, she watched as he came to the table and handed her the glass of water he'd been force-feeding her all night. "Drink. And then go back to sleep. The sun's not even up yet."

She complied, but only because she was too groggy to do anything else. When she'd laid back against the pillows, he adjusted the blankets over her, taking care to cover her arms while making sure her mouth and nose weren't blocked.

Sandro Davies was, she thought, an intriguing study in contrasts.

Very cold, but occasionally hot. Gruff, but tender. A twin, but like no other man she'd ever met.

She fought the exhaustion as best she could, wanting to watch the implacable features on his downturned face and see if he betrayed any feeling, even by accident. Because she knew the feelings were in there. He was like a two-liter bottle of soda, well shaken. Under control for now, but just wait until that lid came off.

"You're staring," he observed, his attention still focused on the blankets.

"I can't help it."

"What do you see?"

"Not Tony."

That got him. His gaze narrowed and zeroed in on her face with sudden urgency, searching for things she hoped he never discovered.

"What does that mean?"

It meant many things, none of which she was prepared to get into right now. Mostly it meant that Sandro affected her a million times more than his brother ever had, and the men were *twins*.

How could that make sense?

"I don't know what it means," she said as a flush crept over her cheeks.

His brows quirked with skepticism, if not downright disbelief. It was no surprise that he wasn't convinced, especially since she was lying through her teeth, but it was still a jolt to be challenged.

"Are you sure about that?" he asked.

She didn't answer.

That persistent knocking was really getting on her nerves.

Skylar groaned, fighting the grogginess and trying her best to get back to the peaceful oblivion she'd just left. There was a beautiful moment of absolute silence, but the second she began to relax, there it was again:

Knock knock knock.

It was getting louder and harder to ignore, which was really upsetting. If it continued, she'd have to open her eyes.

Knock knock knock.

That did it. With a Herculean effort, she struggled against the warmth of the linens, batting them away, and cracked her lids open a tiny slit.

What the—?

Full consciousness slammed into her. Levering up on her elbows, she took in the room with a sweeping glance.

First thing? She was no longer on the leather sofa in the study. No. She was in a pale blue bedroom that looked as though it'd been ripped straight from the pages of *Architectural Digest* magazine. The wall opposite the bed wasn't a wall at all, but a row of floor-to-ceiling windows that were currently covered with the kind of handmade silken Roman shades that probably cost ten grand per window. Even with the shades down, though, the room was bright with natural light, telling her that it was way late, possibly past noon.

There was a seating area in front of another smaller fireplace, which had a blazing fire spreading heat better than a radiator ever could. There were lamps, chairs, tables and ottomans. There was a wardrobe, a dresser and a dressing table, and a pair of crutches leaning against the dressing table. There were two open doors, one of which led to a bathroom, the other to a walk-in closet.

Knock knock knock.

"Hello? Are you alive in there?" called a voice.

Oh, but the surprises didn't end with the room. There was more: she was in a bed. A four-poster so high that it needed—yep, there it was—a stool to climb into, made all the higher by the luxury flowered linens piled atop her.

But the biggest surprise of all was her attire. Rather than Sandro's T-shirt, she was now wearing—she looked down at her body, gasping in disbelief—her own Victoria's Secret full-length pink-cotton nightgown, the one with spaghetti straps and triangle cups. The same nightgown that had last resided in her overnight bag, which was, in turn, in the trunk of the smashed car. The bag that was now, she saw, neatly sitting in the corner near the wardrobe.

Her e-reader, which she'd charged before she came, had been thoughtfully placed on the nightstand.

Being smarter than the average bear, she added up all the evidence and came to one inescapable conclusion: Sandro had, sometime this morning, carried her up here, undressed and redressed her, and arranged her in this bed, all without waking her.

Unbelievable.

Knock knock knock. "Hello," called that exasperated voice again. "I'm coming in to make sure you're not dead—"

"Who is it?" she cried, yanking up the bedding under her chin.

"Nikolas," came the reply.

Nikolas? Who the hell was—

"Nikolas Davies?" said the voice. "Sandro's kid?"

Oh! Nikolas! Of course!

"Sorry!" she said, swiping a hand through her rat's nest of hair. "Come in."

The door swung open and Skylar tried not to gape.

Nikolas walked in with a bed tray held in one hand.

Actually, he didn't walk so much as he...slunk. Which may be the only way to ambulate when the waistband of your baggy jeans only came up to the bottom half of your butt—she sure hoped his poor belt never gave out, because otherwise they'd all be seeing a lot more of this kid's paisley silk boxers—and the bottom four inches of the legs pooled behind the flapping tongue of your boat-size athletic shoes.

He was tall but lanky, having grown into his height but not his musculature, and he possessed a younger version of his father's face, which made him quite handsome.

All resemblance ended there.

He wore an unbuttoned plaid shirt over a T-shirt that said, in big letters, "Don't Hate," and he had at least four glittering studs running up the rim of one ear. The end of one of his heavy black eyebrows had been shaved and now consisted of three or four stripes, and his hair was… interesting. He sported a Mr. T mohawk of unruly dark curls, and the back half of it was—honest to God—red.

His glittering eyes were pure attitude, although she could tell he was putting on his polite expression for the houseguest. For now.

Wow. She could just imagine how this rebel youngling went over with his straight-as-an-arrow, former-soldier father.

Can you say *World War III?*

Reaching the side of the bed, he nodded down at her and gave her one of those hard teenage stares. "'S up?"

Skylar made a quick decision to play it cool. This kid was clearly all about shock value; ergo, she would not be shocked by anything he said or did.

So she adjusted herself into a sitting position against the pillows, ignored the throbbing complaint in her side and leg, and stuck out her hand. "Hi, Nikolas. Great to meet you. I'm Skylar."

"Hey."

Nikolas had a deep voice, a firm grip and great eye

contact, which put him way ahead of many of the mumbling teenagers she had crossed paths with in her practice.

"My dad said you're a vet. He told me to call you Dr. Lawrence."

She snorted. "Oh, well, if the Captain told you to call me Dr. Lawrence, then you need to call me Sky. He'll love that."

His brows (brow and a half?) rose in surprise, and he treated her to part of a begrudging smile before he caught himself and reverted to sulky.

"So you're…what? Thirteen?"

He shrugged. "Yeah."

"Eighth grade?"

"Yeah."

"Do you go to school here in Sagaponack?"

Uh-oh. Wrong question. His face tightened down.

"Not an option. I board. My dad prefers me as far away as possible."

There was a world of bitterness there, so much that it made her heart ache for both father and son. She studied him hard, trying to get another bead on him.

"I'm thinking you're not the sports type. Which means you must be in a band. Or a rapper. Which is it?"

He stood a little straighter, fighting that reluctant smile again. "I paint. A little. And I'm a drummer. In a, ah, drum circle."

"*Drum Circle?* No way! I saw one of those at Faneuil Hall back in Boston last summer. All these drummers just, I don't know, came together and started riffing off each other. It was amazing. Do you play djembe or doumbek or…"

He hesitated, clearly trying not to show his surprise that she knew the names. "Ah…both."

"I'd love to hear you play sometime. Maybe before I leave?"

"Ah…sure."

"What about the piano I saw? Who plays?"

"My, ah, dad used to, but he hasn't in a long time."

"Oh." That made her sad, for reasons she couldn't identify. "So…is there anything on that tray for me to eat? I'm starving."

"What? Oh. Yeah." Taking great care, he lowered it onto her lap. "Here you go."

Her stomach had launched into an urgent growl—she hadn't eaten anything since she had had a protein bar in the car yesterday afternoon—so she had high hopes for a hearty meal. And then she saw a cup of milk, a spoon and a bowl filled with a bunch of rainbow-colored sugar chips. No bacon, no eggs or toast, not even a glass of orange juice or a banana.

Was this what they fed this growing boy for breakfast?

"Hope you like Fruity Bites," he said.

Skylar didn't miss a beat. "I love them," she said, grinning and pouring the milk, which she sincerely hoped wasn't sour, because God knew how often this motley crew made it to the grocery store.

"Good. It was either that or the leftover pizza from the other night."

"Take-out pizza? I'd've thought people living in a house like this would have a housekeeper and cook or something."

Another shrug. "We did, but she retired at the beginning of the year. Dad hasn't found anyone else yet. So let's just say we're not gaining a lot of weight around here."

"Well, that stinks. Oh, hang on. The power's still out, isn't it?"

"Yeah. The whole area's dark. And we haven't seen sign of repair crews or anything yet—"

"Which means my car is still buried under that monster tree."

"You got it."

"What time is it, by the way?"

"Almost two."

"In the afternoon?"

"Yep."

"Wow." She took a bite of cereal, feeling the zing of sugar shoot straight to her brain. "Hey, this is pretty good. I might need another bowl."

"You got it."

Nikolas sauntered off toward the door, but she couldn't let him go without an answer to the question that was burning inside her, refusing to be ignored.

"Where's, ah, Sandro?"

"Hell if I know. We do better when we stay out of each other's way."

O-kay. That didn't sound good.

"But that reminds me." Nikolas snapped his fingers and swung back around to the bed. Shoving a hand into his back pocket, he produced a folded piece of ivory stationery and handed it to her. "He wanted me to give you this."

A note? But where was Sandro? Not that she expected him to continue his vigil over her—of course not!—but she had, inexplicably, gotten used to having him around.

Fighting a sinking feeling of disappointment, she read the note.

Skylar—
Eat. Rest. Read. Use the old set of crutches to go to the bathroom. Behave. Those are orders.
A
P.S. You won't be getting out of here for another day or two at the earliest. The roads are a mess. Sorry.

Aaaaaaand…that was it. No word about where he was or when he'd be back. The disappointment blossomed.

Disgruntled, she flopped back against the pillows. Now what?

Well, she wasn't going to mope around in this gloomy sick room, waiting for Mr. Warm and Fuzzy to reappear and bless her with his caustic presence, that was for sure. Some sunshine would do her good.

"Hey," she said.

Nikolas, who was on the move again and had almost made it to the door, paused, head cocked.

"Could you please open the shades for me?"

"Sure thing."

He went to work on the cords and she turned back to her cereal, digging into it like a rabid wolverine. It was a good thing she'd had the whole week scheduled off; this way she wouldn't miss any appointments and make her staff crazy trying to find her. As soon as the cell towers were back online—or maybe the electric would come on first—she'd send a couple texts or emails just to let everyone know—where she was.

"There you go," Nikolas disappeared out the door. "I'll get you more cereal."

"Thanks." She looked up from her cereal. "I really appreciate— Oh, my God."

The view outside her huge windows was spectacular. Breathtaking. A stretch of green lawn yielded to a covered pool surrounded by swaying sea grasses that were trimmed, brown and dormant for the winter. More grasses formed a wall, on the other side of which was a debris-strewn stretch of beach that extended farther than her eyes could see. Beyond that was the sparkling ocean, still turbulent after the big storm, but a blinding blue that reflected the day's clear skies and bright sun.

Light flooded the room, making it so cheerful that she couldn't believe how last night's forbidding and dark mausoleum could inhabit anything this warm and lovely.

And she wondered, again, about the many sides of Sandro Davies, the man who'd almost become her brother-in-law.

Chapter 6

She showed up at ten-thirty that night, which was later than Sandro had expected. On the other hand, he'd prayed she wouldn't come at all, so maybe this was the best outcome he could hope for.

He'd known, on some gut level, that giving Skylar the widest possible berth until she left his house—he hated to think he was *avoiding* her; that made him seem like such a coward—wouldn't take care of the problem she presented. Actually, *problem* was the wrong word.

Temptation. That was the right word.

The good thing was, she gave him plenty of warning that she was on her way. Hobbled with her bad leg and the crutches, she'd thumped down the staircase like a kangaroo on a Pogo stick, and then roamed up and down the long hallways, tapping on the various doorways with her discreet knock, looking for him in the dark and quiet house. Now here she was.

He looked up from his book and stared at the fire's dancing flames, waiting, his pulse a hard beat of anticipation in his throat.

She knocked.

He paused, torn between the right choice and what he wanted, which never seemed to be the same thing. Why should tonight be any different?

"Come in," he called, choosing what he wanted, which was to see her. Just for a little while, and only because he hadn't seen her today. Where was the harm?

The door swung open, and there she was, in all her injured glory, her face flushed with effort and her eyes bright with excitement.

God, she was beautiful.

He studied her under cover of the shadows, approving of what he saw. Her hair was in what looked like a damp ponytail, with curls falling across her forehead and over her ears. She'd changed into a long-sleeve T-shirt and a pair of those sleek black exercise pants (for yoga, weren't they?) that emphasized the lean curves of her hips and thighs. Her pretty bare feet, with dark polish, were in black flip-flops, and her injured leg was pulled up, so that only her toes grazed the floor. Her leg didn't seem to be unduly swollen or painful.

"Hi," she said.

"Hi."

"Can I come in?"

"Could I stop you?"

Grinning, she didn't bother to answer, but swung all the way into the room, shutting the door behind her. It took her a few hopping steps before she made it to the chair nearest his spot on the sofa and collapsed. Her restless gaze touched everything in his den: the neutral upholstery, the glass tables, the brass floor lamps, the fire, the flat-screen TV mounted above the mantel, the candles, his battery-operated book light, his book.

Her curiosity satisfied, she turned back to him. "Man cave, eh?"

"Apparently not."

Skylar was, he'd discovered, impervious to hints and verbal darts, and this one, naturally, rolled right off her protective shell.

"Good news," she announced. "I'm doing better."

"I heard." He'd had regular updates on her progress from Mickey.

"And even though you couldn't be bothered to come see me all day—"

"I was outside, clearing the smaller branches from the road."

"—I thought you'd want to know that I don't have a fever and the stitches are holding. And my leg isn't that swollen, which is good."

"Excellent."

"I took a nap and a shower."

"Great."

"Mickey brought me dinner."

"The peanut butter and jelly was to your liking?"

"It was delicious. But I prefer blackberry jam over grape jelly."

"I'll make a note. Anything else? Before you head back to your room, where you belong?"

"Yes. I met Nikolas. I like him. He seems like a great kid."

Was she joking? "Really?"

"Really. You don't agree?"

"Let's just say that the headmasters of the last two schools that expelled him didn't agree."

"So he has some issues, but what teenager doesn't? He'll be fine."

"And you base this on... What? Your experience raising your goldfish?"

"I don't have a goldfish."

"And you don't have kids, either, so I'm not sure you know what you're talking about."

"Maybe not," she said brightly, "but this is America, where everyone's entitled to an opinion."

"Ah, but I don't have to listen to it. Especially in my own house."

"The thing is," she continued, "I'm wondering if he wants to spend more time with you. Maybe that's what he needs. You know?"

"I don't know."

"I think maybe the reason you don't get along is because you don't spend enough time together. I know it sounds counterintuitive, but I really think that could be the problem."

"Who says there's a problem?"

She stared at him with those clear, dark eyes, saying nothing but seeing everything. If there was judgment there, she didn't show it, but it didn't matter. He was his own harshest critic, and he'd already condemned himself to hell and back for screwing up on the fatherhood thing. Between his long stints overseas and his complete inability to understand anything about his own kid, he was a regular paternal genius. Hell, if he kept doing such a great job, the boy would be in prison by Christmas.

Finally, he had to drop his gaze. Discomfort made him scrub his hand over his jaw, which she undoubtedly noticed.

"I'm thinking that being a single parent to a surly teenage boy is harder than leading a company of soldiers," she said softly, catching him off guard.

He was good at a lot of things, but admitting weakness and showing emotion weren't on that particular list and probably never would be. After all, what soldier was touchy-feely? Except that there was so much gentle understanding in Skylar's expression that he couldn't stop himself from opening up to her. Or maybe he was merely accepting the hand of friendship she'd extended him. The bottom line was: it was hard not to meet her halfway.

"I'm thinking you're right," he admitted.

She nodded. "Can I ask you a question?"

He shrugged.

"You love his hair, don't you?"

One stunned beat passed, and then he grinned. Before he knew it, the grin had progressed to a chuckle, and then he and Skylar were laughing together. At least until she abruptly stopped laughing and started staring.

"What?" he demanded.

"I didn't think you could smile, much less laugh."

She was right, but the observation still irritated him. Unsettled him. Because why was his dead brother's former fiancée so attuned to him and his moods?

Why did everything about this woman throw him off-kilter?

Was she feeling this…this attraction thing between them like he was? Did he affect her breathing the way she affected his? Why did the desire to touch her feel like it would suffocate him if it wasn't satisfied soon?

Why couldn't he explain the hold she had over him?

Maybe she knew his thoughts were spiraling out of control, because she pointed to his book and changed the subject. "What're you reading?"

His memory failed him, forcing him to look at the spine. "It's about Crazy Horse and Custer."

"So you like biographies?"

"I like military histories."

"Figures. I didn't think you were the science-fiction type."

Well, she was right about that, too. Damn woman. What did she like to read? More importantly, why did he care about the minutiae of her life? His mouth opened, ready to ask her, and that was when he caught himself.

What did he think he was doing here with the woman Tony had loved? Was his honor so depleted that he could now justify spending time alone with her in this cozy little nest? And if he reached for her…kissed her… touched her…would he justify that, as well?

What kind of a man had he become?

Unbidden and unwelcome, a memory of Tony barged into his mind.

Sandro stared at Tony, trying to analyze his crazy grin. "What the hell's gotten into you?"

Tony turned several shades of purple, dropped his head in a hangdog gesture, and ran a hand over his nape. "I, ah—I'm seeing someone."

Sandro snorted. Was that all? Was her shit made of emeralds, or what? "And?"

Tony looked up again, serious now, sporting the kind of ecstatic inner glow that could only mean one thing. Sandro felt the kick of understanding in his gut even before Tony spoke again.

"I'm going to marry her, man."

"How do you know?"

"I don't know. You'd have to meet her. I can't explain it."

"Sandro?"

Sandro blinked and there she was, the woman who'd enthralled his brother, staring at him with concern in those incredible eyes.

The woman who, let's face it, enthralled him.

Which made him a twisted SOB.

He stood abruptly, desperate to get rid of her so he could clear his mind and, hopefully, breathe again. So what if he was being rude? Striding to the door, he opened it for her.

"It's time for you to go back to bed, and I need to find out how the Battle of Little Big Horn turned out," he announced. "So don't let me keep you."

Hurt flashed across her face, and he felt a responsive squeeze of pain in his chest. "You're not subtle, are you?"

"Subtle wouldn't work with you, Skylar."

Maybe she knew she was showing too much emotion, because she looked away, nodded and made a production out of getting to her feet and balancing on the crutches. He felt the strong urge to help her, but keeping some distance between them seemed like a good idea right now. And, anyway, she would demand to do it herself. She was stubborn that way.

A few quick strides put her right at the door, right in his face, and she'd brought all of her delicious scents with her. The apple-fresh trace of shampoo; the hint of flowers, maybe from her lotion; the indefinable fragrance that only the warmth of her skin could generate.

She paused, looking up at him. "Thank you for taking such good care of me last night."

Why was she so close?

Agonized, he stared down at her, trying to get his lungs to work, but not too well, because if he breathed her in the way he wanted to, he'd probably become an instant addict. He also tried to stay outside the radius of her body heat and tried not to contemplate how well her tender lips would fit against his.

And then he provided them both with a badly needed reminder.

"Tony would have wanted me to keep you safe."

She hesitated, a flare of annoyance making her jaw tighten. "Would Tony have wanted you to handle my naked body when you put me into my nightgown?"

He stilled. She was goading him, but this wasn't second grade and he should be man enough to ignore the bait.

Should be.

Instead, he stepped closer, his voice dropping even as his pulse spiked, fully engaged in any battle she cared to fight.

"I didn't think you'd complain about being made more comfortable, sweet Sky. And I didn't think your modesty was an issue after that stunt you pulled last night."

Her cheeks colored, and he awarded himself *check* and *mate*.

Prematurely, as it turned out.

Because she tipped up that stubborn chin of hers, and one corner of her perfect, perfect mouth edged back into a knowing woman's smile. Her eyes glittered.

He stared, helpless to do otherwise.

"This is what I want to know," she said in a husky

murmur that raised the hair on his arms. "Did you enjoy it?"

He didn't—couldn't—answer, which was answer enough.

Skylar left. Sandro's tortured thoughts of her lingered, as they had ever since the night he had stumbled upon her at the party here on the estate.

A woman was standing under the far end of the wisteria trellis.

She was leaning, actually, as though she needed the post's support to keep her upright and the leafy overhang to hide her from the flickering torchlight and the other guests at the party.

Her dress was a flutter of white against her caramel skin, her legs long, bare and sexy in heels designed for the sole purpose of making men salivate. Windswept black curls brushed over her shoulders, which were heaving with silent sobs, and she kept her head bowed while she dabbed at her eyes with a tissue.

There were few things he avoided like crying women— drinking the water in a couple of the shit holes where he'd done tours came to mind—and his gut instinct was to creep back into the shadows, make a belated appearance at his brother's engagement party and leave her to her misery, which was, after all, none of his business.

Except that the crunch of the gravel beneath his feet was like the clap of cymbals in the relative silence, and her sudden cringe was a dead giveaway that she knew he was there.

And there was something unidentifiable about her that...

Called to him? Touched him? Pulled him outside himself?

"I don't blame you for crying," he said. "It's not much of a party, is it?"

That got her. To his overwhelming relief, her head came up—he realized she had a white flower tucked behind one ear—and she laughed, swiping at her tears as she turned in his direction.

Whoa.

That first glimpse of her face created an honest-to-God lightning-bolt moment, one that made his thoughts disperse and his breath whoosh out of his lungs. Her smile came and went, flashing a perfect white, and her dark doe's eyes were so brilliant with tears that he meant to look away. Too bad instant paralysis had shut down any possibility of movement.

Deep in his chest, his heart began to thud.

Thankfully, she didn't seem to notice the effect she had on him. She raised her empty flute up to eye level. "I'm out of champagne."

"Someone could probably round up another bottle for you, you know. No need to cry."

Another fleeting laugh did crazy things to his pulse.

"I don't think I need any more tonight. I'm not a pretty drunk."

He'd have to take her word for it because she sure as hell was pretty. He shrugged. "Suit yourself."

He hesitated, undecided.

That was it, wasn't it? He'd stumbled onto a crying woman and made a joke. She'd laughed. Mission accomplished, right? He'd done his random act of kindness for the day. The end.

Well, it wasn't quite the end, but it needed to be.

He was attracted to her, yeah, but a) she was upset and vulnerable; and b) it went without saying that a woman this fine was spoken for.

Bottom line? He should leave.

But...he couldn't leave.

They stared at each other.

"Do you...want to talk about it?" he asked after a minute.

A shadow crossed her expression. She blinked back the last of her tears, and the unexpected intimacy of the last minute or so disappeared with them, leaving two strangers who didn't know anything about each other and probably never would.

"No," she said. Was there a trace of reluctance in her voice, or did he imagine it? "Thanks."

"Suit yourself," he said again, and he knew he wasn't imagining the stab of disappointment he felt. This time, he actually turned to go, which was progress. "Have a good night."

"Unless—"

He wheeled back around, his entire body on alert even before the whole word was out of her mouth. "Unless?"

"Unless you're good with advice."

Honesty forced him to shake his head and warn her away. "The best advice I can give you is that you should ignore my advice."

She grinned again. He stared again. He couldn't help it.

It was her eyes, he thought, transfixed.

There was something extraordinary about her eyes.

And then her grin faded, leaving only a woman with a problem and him with broad shoulders that didn't get much of a workout these days.

"You could try me, though. I help people every now and then. Usually by accident, but still."

She hesitated. He waited, breath held, because this moment felt important even if he couldn't identify why. He was afraid that anything he did, any wrong move, could tip things in the wrong direction, which was any direction that took her away from him.

He wanted her, this crying woman whose name he didn't know.

He wanted her bad.

She stepped closer, tipping up her chin and nailing him right between the eyes with her earnest urgency. "I woke up this morning, and I didn't recognize my life anymore. I'm heading down a path I didn't mean to take. And I can't figure out how I got here."

Sandro waited for more, but there wasn't anything else.

That was it? The big problem that made her cry? Was he missing something?

"Take a different path," he told her.

"It's not that easy—"

"It is that easy. Take a different path. You can do it."

She faltered, the beginnings of a frown creasing her forehead.

A beat or two passed, during which the world shrank around them.

Was she drifting closer? Was he? When had her eyes become the only thing in his field of vision? When had he gotten close enough to feel the warmth of her skin?

"But...I don't want to hurt anyone," she said, low.

He had an impulse to touch her. He didn't try to resist it. Reaching out, he used his thumb to swipe a lingering tear off her cheek.

Once that was done, he discovered that he didn't want to move his fingers away from the sweet satin of her skin.

When she should have moved away, she didn't. When he should have dropped his hand, he couldn't. His attention was riveted on her sparkling eyes...her dewy lips... her words...her... .

Only when he caught himself leaning in and lowering his head did he stop. His body, which was taut with sexual tension, didn't appreciate this late display of gentlemanly behavior. But kissing this woman now wouldn't be the right thing, and he always tried to do the right thing, even when it hurt.

Especially when it hurt.

"If you were on the right path," he said, stepping back

and letting her go, "you wouldn't be out here crying. Would you?"

She shook her head, her gaze still locked with his. When she spoke again, her voice was throaty bordering on hoarse.

"What's your name?"

"Alessandro. Davies."

There was a pause.

A long, awful pause.

Her expression rearranged itself into one of dawning comprehension and...dismay. "Alessandro?"

He, meanwhile, was experiencing his own unwanted epiphany.

He tried to ease into the knowledge, but it was already overwhelming him and congealing into a leaden ball in the pit of his gut.

Pistons fired in his overheated brain; dots connected; phrases replayed.

I'm heading down a path I didn't mean to take. I don't want to hurt anyone—

"What's your name?" he asked, but he knew, even before an unwelcome male voice, the confident voice of his brother, Tony, the man who'd bested him every day of his life, called out.

Tony emerged from the shadows, grinning, flushed and happy.

"Skylar! Where'd you get off to? You're not hiding from me, are you— Ah, I see you met my worse half.

You'll notice I got all the looks in the family. Sandro, this is Skylar, my fiancée."

Tony hooked an arm around Skylar's waist, reeled her in, ran his hand through her hair and kissed her on the very same mouth that Sandro had just been lusting after. Sandro watched it all happen, sickened by a feeling of loss that he couldn't justify and the sudden realization that he was the biggest and stupidest punk in the world.

Skylar broke the kiss first, looking flustered. "Tony—"

"Come on, baby." Tony steered her toward the house and out of Sandro's life. "They want us to cut the cake."

Then they disappeared up the path and were gone, leaving only Skylar's white flower on the gravel at Sandro's feet. Naturally, he picked it up and kept it. Oh, he hated her, but he kept the damn flower.

The day after that, Skylar broke up with Tony.

A month after that, they were back in Afghanistan.

A person could die in a firefight, or in a car accident or in a plane crash. Those were the usual ways. But could memories choke the life out of a person? Sandro wondered. Could longing? Could frustrated desire?

Hands shaking, he reached for the desk drawer and pulled it open. Reached inside. And pulled out Skylar's flower, dried, pressed between the folded note card that had kept it safe when he'd carried it overseas, to the war. He pressed it to his nose, remembering. Yearning.

That was the thing about Skylar: she was with him. She was always with him.

Chapter 7

"Hey, hey, hey!" called a voice behind Skylar early the next morning. "What the hell're you doing there? You trying to get yourself into trouble, or what?"

Damn. And she'd almost made a clean getaway. Not that she'd hoped to get far with her bad leg, which was merely achy today rather than outright painful, but still.

Skylar adjusted her scarf a little higher around her neck and turned to see Mickey rolling down the path toward her, arms pumping and eyes glinting. She'd hoped to sneak out for her little walk and back in again before anyone could warn her against it, but so much for that plan.

"Good morning," she evaded, flashing him a smile

that she hoped looked convincingly innocent. "What a beautiful day."

Mickey, who was wearing fingerless gloves along with his black knit cap and puffy jacket, jabbed his index finger at her. "Don't even try it. I will not be sweet-talked. What the hell are you trying to do to your stitches there? You know I'm not an M.D. Those things could pop any second with you roaming around out here like you're on a freaking hike. Why can't you stay put? What's the matter with you?"

Wow. Those was a lot of questions. "I'm getting a little exercise. And my leg is fine."

"Yeah, well don't expect me to go fixing you up again when you topple over and crack your thick skull. Just so we're clear."

"I understand. Why don't you come with me?"

"The Cap would kill me. I don't get paid for strolling and chatting."

"What, ah, do you get paid for?"

"Groundskeeping. And whatever else he cooks up for me to do."

"Well, the gardens are beautiful. What I can see of them, anyway."

He narrowed his eyes at her, looking suspicious. "Thanks."

"How did you wind up working here?"

"The Cap didn't approve of me trying to drink myself to death after I lost my legs. So he hauled my ass up by the scruff of my neck and put me to work." He shrugged. "Now I got something to do."

"He'd be lost without you. I can tell."

Mickey blinked, frowning.

"So…why don't I make breakfast this morning?" she suggested.

"There ain't nothing to make."

"Didn't you mention you had some milk and eggs in a cooler on ice?"

"Lady, we ain't got no power."

"Don't we have fires in the fireplaces? Where's your sense of adventure?"

His bottom jaw hit his lap. "What do I look like—a camper?"

"Okay, well, look. You can sit there and argue with me, or you can show up at chow time. I've got a taste for French toast and eggs. Assuming you bachelors have some syrup around here somewhere."

He shrugged, his eyes showing a flare of begrudging interest. "I'll get you some syrup."

"Great! I'll meet you in the kitchen in half an hour."

"You got it." He wheeled around to go, but then snapped his fingers and turned back. "The crews're getting closer, clearing the trees and whatnot. They should have the roads clear soon. You hear 'em?"

The relentless buzzing of chainsaws had woken her, even though her room was on the backside of the house. She'd done her best to ignore it. Possibly because she knew that if the roads were being cleared, then her days here were numbered, if not over. And she didn't want to leave the Hamptons yet.

She didn't want to leave Sandro yet.

"I heard them," she said, trying to act like this was good news.

"I thought that would make you happy."

With that, Mickey disappeared toward the house, and she continued her slow hobble down the curve in the path toward the short boardwalk. Not that she was dumb enough to risk the crutches on the sand, but she did want a glimpse of the water.

Hang on. What was that? Was she imagining things, or—

No, there it was again—a glimpse of black among the grasses…the twitches of a long and skinny tail, tipped with white…oh, and look at that face! It was a kitten. No, wait. Two kittens! They peered at her, wide-eyed and skittish behind the shoots of dried grass. Poor little guys. Were they hungry? Where was mama cat? Had they gotten separated during the storm?

She bent at the waist, not daring to test her bad leg by squatting, and held out a welcoming hand.

"Hello, kitties," she sang. "Hell-ooo."

The kittens froze. One of them opened its mouth in a high-pitched mewl that sounded like an accusation.

"Well, excuse me." Skylar took one slow step forward, trying not to scare them away. "I didn't do anything to you. I'm trying to help—"

The next step was one too many, and they scampered accordingly.

"Wait," she called after them, but they were long gone by the time she made it to their hiding place, and their little footprints in the sand disappeared into dense undergrowth.

"Well, that stinks," she muttered.

Making up her mind to keep an eye out for them, she resumed her hobbling progress. The dried grasses tapered off, letting her see farther ahead, and there, stooped over something that was fluttering on the boardwalk, was Nikolas.

Today he wore a dark hoodie (hood pulled up, of course) with baggy shorts that revealed skinny legs and those gunboat-size shoes. Why his teeth weren't chattering with the cold, she had no idea. Maybe today's blue skies and bright sunlight had made him more optimistic about the advent of spring than she was prepared to be just yet.

"Hey," she called, keeping a tight grip on the white planks as she hopped up the four stairs to the walkway. "What's going on? Not another animal? I just saw a couple kittens."

He glanced over his shoulder and scowled at the sight of her. "You're going to land right on your butt."

"I know," she said cheerfully, looking at the squirming pile of feathers at his feet. "What's that? Seagull? No, wait. That's a kingfisher."

His eyes widened. "A kingfisher?"

She leaned closer, checking. It was a handsome bird, about the size of a pigeon, with beady black eyes, a long and sharp black bill, a gray crest and a horizontal gray stripe and wings to contrast with its white belly. There was no brown, which meant—

"Yeah. A male. With a broken wing. That's why his feathers look all crazy."

"*All crazy?* Is that the medical term for it?"

"Yep." She grinned and reached to pick up the bird, giving that sharp beak a wide berth. The bird did not approve and squawked accordingly. "Poor little guy. The storm probably tossed him around. It's okay, little fella. It's o-kaaaay."

"Wait, wait, WAIT. What're you doing?"

"I'm going to take him inside and set his wing. We can't just leave him here."

"You know what you're doing, right?"

She straightened, cradling the bird between her palms and trying to soothe him without suffering a puncture wound from that lethal beak.

"I worked at a zoo one summer when I was in veterinary school. Took care of an ostrich. So I think I can manage this guy."

"Yeah, but ostriches can't fly."

Laughing, she turned to lead the way back toward the house. "Come on. I'll show you how to make a splint. Will you grab my crutches for me and maybe take my arm so I don't fall? Thanks."

Nikolas complied and held her in his firm grip as she

hopped back down the steps, but he didn't look happy about it. "Dad's not going to like this—"

"Oh, so what?" she muttered. "What *does* your dad like, exactly?"

That got a grin out of him. "You're subversive. I like that in a person. I'm still going to throw you under the bus when he demands to know why there's a wild bird in the house, though."

"Honey, I've been attacked by a tree. I'm not scared of your dad."

"You will be," he said in a pretty good Yoda imitation. "You will be. What should we name him?"

The Yoda reference made her think of *Star Wars,* which made her think— "How about Skywalker?"

Nikolas nodded thoughtfully. "That could work." He peered down at the bird's face. "You like that?"

The bird screeched, looking as threatening as he possibly could when only his ruffled head was showing above Skylar's fists.

"Skywalker it is," Nikolas said happily.

The smell of coffee and bacon lured Sandro into the kitchen, where he stood at the threshold and watched the buzz of activity, frozen with stupefaction.

Nikolas and Mickey scurried back and forth around the granite island, shuttling plates, silverware and syrup to the weathered oak table, upon which already sat a glass pitcher of orange juice.

There was a…a…yes, his eyes were not deceiving him…a live bird with a bandaged wing sitting atop the mantelpiece and squawking its fool head off. And there at the stone hearth, stooped over the roaring fire with an iron skillet, was the cause of all this uproar, the thorn in his side and the cross he had to bear, at least for a little while longer—Skylar.

Smiling and pink-faced with excitement, she used a spatula to flip something in the skillet. Was that French toast? Also perched over the fire was a blue enamel coffee pot he'd had no idea they even owned. A stack of bacon, crispy the way he liked it, drained on some paper towels on the counter.

His stomach, which had subsisted on PB and Js and protein bars for the last couple days, rumbled with approval and anticipation.

So Skylar had managed to make a breakfast feast with no power.

That was unusual.

Stranger still? Mickey, who was suspicious of strangers and had never met anyone he wasn't happy to curse out, was cheerfully folding napkins and arranging plates. Meanwhile, Nikolas, he of the perpetual sulky moods, bad attitude and general surliness, was—wait for it— humming.

Yes, *humming.*

Sandro had seen enough. He stepped all the way into the room. "What's going on in here?"

Much to his annoyance, they all gave a little start and stilled, looking around at him with wide eyes, like three little mice who'd been happily playing until the big bad cat came back.

Which made him the big bad cat.

He didn't get it. He was quiet and he had high expectations of himself and others, which meant that he didn't suffer fools, and, yeah, he probably still had that commanding air about him, which came from years of commanding.

But seriously. Did he bring that much gloom with him when he walked into the room?

Why were they all looking at him as though he'd just shot Bambi?

"We're having breakfast," Skylar informed him. "You're welcome to join us."

The *if you're nice* was implied, but he still heard it.

"Why, thank you," he replied. "It's always nice to be invited to sit at my own table."

"Make sure you wash your hands," Skylar said, now flipping the French toast.

"I'm familiar with basic hygiene procedures." He went to the sink and lathered up. "Which reminds me. What the hell is that bird doing on the mantel?"

Skylar, who had moved on to transferring the finished French toast to a platter, shot the bird a fond glance. "This is Skywalker. He's a belted kingfisher. His wing is broken from the storm."

Sandro slid into his place on the bench at the table, opposite Nikolas. "I didn't ask about his demographics. I'm wondering who installed him in the house and why."

Shrugging, Skylar gave him a sweet smile that was at complete odds with the subtle defiance flashing in her eyes. "I figured that you were the kind of guy who'd want to help a vulnerable creature. Was I wrong?"

Well, now what the hell was he supposed to say to that?

He stared at her, wondering how much strategic training she'd had to outflank him so easily. With his four years at West Point and lengthy army career, he'd thought he'd be a match for one small woman, but apparently he'd miscalculated.

"And how long will this vulnerable creature be pooping on the mantel?" he wondered.

"Not too long. Unless you have a cage? I didn't see a cage."

A *cage?* Was she for real?

He was still gaping at her when he caught a movement out of the corner of his eye. Since he was anxious to exit this unwinnable discussion with Skylar as soon as possible, he turned, only to discover Mickey passing in his wheelchair, craning his neck to look at him with way too much amusement in his face.

"I'll fire your ass," Sandro warned him. "Just give me a reason."

Mickey snorted back a laugh. "Just checking to see how many pieces of bacon you want, Cap."

"I'll have my portion and your portion."

"Aye, Cap," Mickey said, continuing on his way.

"Here we go." Skylar arrived at the table with the platter, which she passed around once she'd taken a place next to Sandro on the bench. "I hope everyone's—"

They descended on the platter like snarling hyenas. Mickey and Sandro took four pieces of French toast apiece; Nikolas took six. They each grabbed a handful of bacon, and Mickey and Nikolas both reached across the table for the pitcher, nearly knocking it over in their haste. Mickey smacked Nikolas's hand away and grabbed it.

"—Hungry," Skylar finished, looking a little revolted.

"Thanks for the chow, ma'am." Mickey stuck an entire slice of bacon in his mouth and reached for more on the platter. "It sure is tasty."

"Now wait one minute." Skylar snatched the platter away, glaring at them all in turn. Nikolas looked up from his plate and waited, a huge piece of French toast suspended on his fork halfway to his mouth. Sandro put the syrup down. "Don't you clowns know we're supposed to take the time to thank the Lord and grace the food?"

Sandro felt the corner of his mouth twitch with a smile, which he repressed. "Does the Lord approve of you calling us clowns?"

Ignoring this, she glowered at him for a second before grabbing his hand, reaching across the table for Mickey's hand, bowing her head and closing her eyes.

"Dear Lord," she began, "please bless this food and all the hands that prepared it."

Since he'd seen too much ugliness in Afghanistan and lost too many valuables (his men; his career; his brother;

his soul), Sandro didn't have much to say to God. Instead of listening to the prayer, he focused on something much more interesting: the feel of Skylar's hand in his.

The delight he took in touching her was wrong, and he knew it. Muddying the waters between them any further was also wrong, and he'd meant to keep his attraction to her on lockdown so he didn't send her any mixed messages.

And he tried; he really did.

The record needed to reflect the effort he put into doing the right thing. For one agonizing second, he stared down at her hand atop his and did nothing other than note the contrast between his dark skin and her caramel skin, his blunt-tipped fingers and her tapered, delicate ones, and the warmth of her body.

"Oh, and thank You for keeping us safe from the storm the other night, and for letting Nikolas find Skywalker. Please let his little wing heal quickly, Lord, and let—"

And then Sandro caved, because some fights couldn't be won.

In one subtle move, his flipped his hand over so that they were palm to palm, but that wasn't enough. So he laced their fingers together and held on tight, rubbing his thumb over the fine skin on the back of her hand, marking every vein and bone.

Her lids flew open and he heard the sudden hitch in her breath.

It was stunning. The contact, the fit, the heat—all of it.

Absolutely mind-blowing.

"—And, ah, we ask all of this in the, ah, name of Your son, our Savior. Amen."

They all stirred, raising their heads and opening their eyes, but he was already on the move. He dropped her hand as though it was a live grenade, surged to his feet and slid off the bench.

What the hell was he doing?

"Is there any blackberry jam?" He headed to the pantry with no real awareness of anything except the haunting intensity of her bewildered gaze as it continued to skewer him between the shoulder blades. "French toast needs blackberry jam."

Chapter 8

They attacked their plates—the men did, anyway—with only their appreciative smacking and grunting to break the silence. It was so great to have a homemade meal that was both hot and delicious that it took Sandro a moment to realize that Skylar was not shoveling it down like they were. She was, in fact, eyeing them with wary amusement.

"There is more," she told them. "So you can take the time to chew."

"Put me down for more," Nikolas said around a mouthful.

"Me, too," Mickey said, slurping orange juice.

Skylar laughed—she had a great laugh, husky and earthy—and hunkered down over her plate, protecting it with her arms. "You're not getting mine, though. So make sure you steer clear."

"No promises," Nikolas said.

The two of them grinned across the table at each other like old pals, which was a shocker. Not because Nikolas liked Skylar, but because Nikolas was smiling. When had he last done that in Sandro's presence? Six months ago? Longer?

"This is great," Sandro told Skylar. "Thank you."

"My pleasure. It's the least I can do after you've taken care of me."

"True," Sandro said.

She reached for her coffee, laughing. "On the other hand, I was injured on your property, so you can expect to hear from my lawyer when I get out of here."

"Seems to me you assumed the risk when you went out into the storm." Sandro slathered more jam on his French toast and swirled a slice of bacon on it. "Not the brightest idea you ever had."

"You may have a point," Skylar said.

"And speaking of you getting out of here, the crew is working on our tree next. I walked down there this morning to check on their progress. So you won't be stuck much longer."

"Funny," she said. "I don't feel stuck. I've never been in such a beautiful house."

Was the house beautiful? It'd been so long since he'd had any pleasure here that it was hard to tell. "Thanks."

"It must take a lot of work, though. A house this age, right on the shore."

"It does." He looked across at Nikolas, who was chugging orange juice like he was at a keg party. "And that reminds me. After we eat, I'll need your help cleaning the muck and debris away from the pool and garden—"

"Wait—*what?*" Horror made Nikolas's jaw drop. He thunked his glass on the table and swiped his wet mouth with the back of his hand.

The kid was a disaster. "Napkin," Sandro muttered.

Nikolas, as usual, ignored him. "Why do I have to help with that crap? That's Mickey's job, isn't it?"

"Hey!" Mickey reached out and smacked him on the back of his head. "Have some manners with your old man, why don't ya?"

"Hey!" Nikolas raised his arms to fend him off.

"Thanks, Mick," Sandro said. "But I'll be the one to physically abuse my son."

"Well, get to it!" Mickey said.

Sandro shot him a *shut the hell up* look and turned back to his son, who was, as far as he was concerned, the root of all problems in this house. "I know you're busy, what with school being canceled and sleeping until noon and whatnot, but in case you missed it, we got hit with a major storm and the property is a mess. We all need to help."

"I had plans!" Nikolas cried.

Sandro stared at him. "How is that possible since you're grounded and, even if you weren't grounded, the roads are blocked and you and your thuggish friends don't have a helicopter at your disposal?"

"I was going to practice my drums this afternoon! You *know* that!"

Sandro shrugged, feeling his blood pressure tick higher and wondering, for the billionth time, how he'd raised a kid who was both this lazy and this ungrateful. "Well, tragic though this will be for music lovers worldwide, you can put your music on the shelf for a little while and practice later."

Nikolas huffed and shoved his plate away, rattling the silver. "Unbelievable!"

"That I have a son this lazy?" Sandro wondered. "Yeah. It is."

"Mom never made me do stuff like that."

"I know. And look how well you've turned out so far."

"My friends don't have to put up with this kind of crap, either!"

Like that was persuasive. Please. Relaxing his scowl, Sandro worked hard on keeping a lid on his spiking temper. Why didn't this kid know when to shut up? Why couldn't he show even the most basic amount of respect for his father? Why'd he have to try to make Sandro look like a punk in front of Skylar?

"Your friends are a bunch of spoiled rich kids who wouldn't know a hard day's work if it bit them in the ass. Luckily for you, you've got me to straighten you out and make sure you become a contributing member of society."

"Yeah, well, I'm not doing it. I'll practice first, and then I'll—"

What? Did this knucklehead actually think he'd get away with telling Sandro *no?*

"Enough," Sandro roared, smacking his palms on the table and making all the plates rattle. "We're going outside in ten minutes, and if you're not there—"

"I'm not sure what your father's about to say, Nikolas," Skylar interjected quietly, "but we've got some thawing steaks that I'd planned to grill for dinner later. Only those males who've worked up a sweat will be served. Got it? Thanks. Now help me with these dishes."

With that, she stood, stacked a bunch of plates and limped toward the sink.

Nikolas stared after her, still fuming.

"Let's go," Skylar said, now running water.

"Fine," Nikolas grumbled. "Shit."

If Nikolas had thought she couldn't hear him, he was sadly mistaken. Skylar turned off the water, turned to stare at Nikolas over her shoulder, and raised one delicate eyebrow. "What did you say?"

Nikolas shrank back like a startled turtle. "Ah…nothing."

"Ma'am," Sandro supplied, working hard to stifle his grin. On the one hand, he was irritated to be shown up, yet again, by this injured woman. On the other hand, anyone who shrank The Beast down to size without yelling was a hero in his book.

"Ma'am," Nikolas added. Hustling now, he stacked plates and grabbed silverware, making a racket.

Skylar frowned. "Don't you break anything."

"No," Nikolas said, heading for the sink. "Ma'am."

Across the table, Sandro and Mickey grinned at each other.

Whoa.

All of a sudden, Skylar didn't feel so hot, which was what she got for making like Wonder Woman, taking a walk and then the whole breakfast thing. Her head waited until the menfolk trooped outside for yard cleanup before it started protesting, which was just as well because she didn't want anyone fussing and acting like she was an invalid. She wasn't. She just needed a nap.

After a final kitchen wipe down and a quick check on Skywalker—who'd finally stopped screeching, fluffed out his feathers and buried his beak in his chest for a rest—she headed into the foyer toward the stairs and—

Whoa.

The room did a pirouette.

Pressing a hand to her head in a vain attempt to master the sudden dizziness, she decided against the stairs. Maybe the chair right here was a better option.

"Skylar."

Feet thundered down the stairs, adding to her general feeling of wooziness, and then Sandro came into view, his eyes so wide and alarmed you'd think she had a hatchet buried in her skull.

"You okay? I knew you were doing too much, chasing after birds and cooking food and who knows what else. No one told you to get carried away. You need to sit down."

As usual, any suggestion of weakness pissed her off. "I am sitting down, genius," she snapped. She smacked his hands away when he tried to assist her as she rose from the chair and began a slow hobble to the living-room sofa, where she could stretch out. "If you want to help, why don't you get me a glass of water?"

"Skylar—"

She pointed to the kitchen. "Go. And hurry up about it."

With a harsh sigh and several dark mutterings that included words like *stubborn, pain in the ass* and *hard-headed,* he strode into the kitchen just as her strength gave out. She collapsed onto the sofa in a heap, closed her eyes, and fought back the aches and pains.

After a second, she began to relax. Better. That was better.

"Here." Sandro was back, taking up his usual post on the sofa at her hip. "Drink this. And I brought you some Tylenol."

Oh, thank God. She was not, for once, planning to argue.

Sitting up, she took the pills and drank her water like an obedient patient, and he watched her the whole time in a taut silence.

"Thanks," she murmured, laying her head back on the pillow and closing her eyes. "Don't worry. I'm okay."

"I don't think you are."

"Don't you have yard work to do?"

"You're not going to die on my watch, are you, Sky?"

There was a little too much urgency in his voice now, much more than the situation warranted. Though her throbbing head didn't like it, she looked up at him and saw, in his stark expression, all the loss he'd endured as a combat veteran, and all the grief. How many times in his life had he sat with someone who was injured, perhaps dying? How much tragedy had he seen? And here she'd scared him again.

"No." Holding his gaze until he began to breathe easier, she smiled as much as her tired body would allow. "I'm not going to die on you."

He tried to smile back. "Good."

They stared at each other. He was way too close, leaning over her in a protective stance, with one of his arms braced on the back of the sofa over her. His worried tension was gone, but another kind of tension was building within him, strong enough for her to feel it. It was the two warring sides of his nature, she realized, his honorable half—or maybe it was simply the wounded half that had seen too much in the war—and the half that wanted her.

She now knew, beyond question, that he did want her.

It burned in his eyes every time he looked at her.

"I should—" his focus dipped, lingering on her mouth "—I should get going. They're waiting for me outside."

"Okay."

"You'll stay put, right? I don't want you to get it into your head to climb up on the roof and replace the damaged shingles, or anything like that."

"No," she promised.

"Good."

He started to get up.

"Sandro," she said.

He waited, a muscle ticking in his jaw. "Yes?"

Don't leave me. Touch me. Kiss me. Forget that I was ever with Tony; that was all a mistake, anyway.

If only she were brave enough to share all of that.

"I...I'm a PK. A preacher's kid. Did you know that?"

His brow quirked. "Ah...no."

"My dad was a strict disciplinarian. Everything I did was a reflection on him, and the congregation was watching."

Sandro stilled, saying nothing to this non sequitur.

"I didn't appreciate the demands. So I dyed my hair jet black. Became a Goth princess. Snuck out at night. Drank. Are you getting the picture?"

Sandro said nothing; even his breathing and blinking seemed suspended.

"Everything I did, for years, was in reaction to his disapproval. It wasn't about me being a bad person. It was about me needing something from him that he never gave me. That's how teenagers are."

"I, ah—" Sandro looked away, clearing his gruff throat. "My whole life, I've only been good at one thing.

Being a soldier. Then I got injured in the explosion that killed Tony, and now—"

"I understand."

His head whipped back around, and there was a fragile glimmer of hope in his eyes. "You do?"

"Yes. But now is your chance to reinvent yourself and learn how to be good at other things."

That intense gaze of his softened, creating sexy little crinkles at the corners of his eyes. Displaying the tenderness that she'd come to expect from him, he stood, grabbed a fringed blanket from the back of the nearest chair, and arranged it over her.

"Close your eyes, Sky," he told her. "Take a nap."

She drifted off, thinking that when he looked at her like that, she could almost believe that she mattered to him. A lot.

"This should do it," the foreman, or whoever he was, said late that afternoon, signaling to the person operating the cherry picker, or whatever that truck thing was. "Bring it this way."

Skylar, Sandro, Nikolas and Mickey were gathered at the end of the driveway, watching the proceedings from a safe distance. Several hard-hat and reflective-vest-wearing workers had descended on the tree midafternoon, wielding chainsaws, ladders and all manner of other dangerous equipment, including a vicious wood chipper that looked like it could dispose of an entire log cabin in under ten seconds.

After several hours of work, they'd pruned and whittled the offending branch, and were now poised to lift it off the car with the crane thingy. Soon, the road would be clear and Skylar could be driven to a car rental or airport, so she could escape back to Boston, where she belonged.

All of which should be great news.

Except that the idea of leaving here—leaving Sandro—filled her with a growing dread that tiptoed right along the edge of despair. If only she had a little more time for...

For what, Skylar?

She didn't know.

If she left now, would she ever see him again?

Would never seeing him again be the worst thing that could happen to her, or the best?

If she stayed...if she stayed...if she stayed, then...

What, Skylar?

Her mind's eye squinted, peering into the future, but it was shapeless and dark, as scary as the overgrown path into the woods in Disney movies.

It didn't make sense, and she couldn't explain it; all she knew was that, for now, she belonged here.

No, that wasn't it.

She belonged with Sandro. That was it.

As though he sensed her turmoil, Sandro glanced down at her.

"We'll have you out of here in no time, Skylar," he murmured.

He wasn't smiling, but there was a gleam of something in his eyes, and she read it as grim triumph. Because weren't they in a battle here, she and Sandro, and weren't they hunkered down in their positions?

Her job was to wear him down, break through his resistance, get him to overcome his misguided sense of honor and admit that he wanted her more than he wanted to be true to Tony's memory.

His job, on the other hand, was to hold his line until he could get rid of her, and then he could go back to his brooding and lonely life.

And what did all that mean?

It came down to this, she decided.

If she won, then they both won.

If he won, then all was lost, for both of them.

Then why was she being coy and beating around the bush? How many chances did she think she was going to get if she didn't break out of her comfort zone sometime soon?

Sometime...like now?

Bolstered by her growing determination, she looked him dead in the eye. "You don't want me out of here," she said, "and we both know it."

Something unidentifiable flared in his expression—Surprise? Panic? Passion?—and then a shout from one of the men jarred them back to their surroundings.

"Look out!"

For one suspended second, nothing happened. Skylar and the others glanced wildly around, trying to come up to speed and wondering what the alarm was for. The branch was off the car, dangling at the end of the crane, and there was nothing terrifying about that.

Only it wasn't the branch that was the problem. It was the trunk.

The workers scrambled for cover.

With a protesting groan of splintering wood and pulled roots, the damaged tree tipped, falling across the road. It took forever for the huge oak to crash, as though it didn't want to let go of the earth and its life.

She watched with utter disbelief as it landed with an endless shudder of branches that sprayed water in every direction and reverberated in the ground beneath their feet. The massive and muddy root ball was the last to settle, with blackened tips dangling like octopus tentacles at the far end.

They all stood there in astonished silence, surveying the damage.

The smashed car was now free, but they were otherwise right back where they started, with the road blocked by several tons of tree. Even the rescue equipment was on the wrong side for any getaways.

Skylar blinked and realized, with a flash of purest joy, that that tree had just bought her another day or two right here where she was, with Sandro.

Judging by his thunderous expression, Sandro knew it, too.

Their gazes locked, and she felt the thrum of electricity prickle over her skin and pool deep in her belly.

"Interesting," she said. "I guess it's not quite time for me to leave, after all, is it?"

She walked off before he could answer.

Chapter 9

Sandro went inside and took a quick shower that did nothing to help him decompress from his growing agitation. He was so full of Skylar—the way she looked, smelled and smiled, not to mention the alarming new fact that she wasn't leaving yet—that he couldn't sit still.

He felt crowded and tight, as though she was inside his skin with him and there was nowhere for him to go and no avenue of escape that wouldn't do him serious physical damage.

It was getting so that the thought of her staying crazed him more than the thought of her leaving and—

No.

He wouldn't go down that road. Not ever, if he could help it, and certainly not now. They'd passed a point of no return, he and Skylar, and his sanity now seemed to be inextricably intertwined with the need to never examine his feelings for her.

What if he discovered that he was falling for her?

What kind of man survived the explosion that'd killed his brother, and then became involved with his brother's woman?

He had just enough honor left to know that he wasn't willing to be that man.

So his plan was really simple: he'd continue to avoid her while she was here (as much as she'd allow, anyway), she'd leave as soon as possible, and life would, eventually, revert to normal.

Otherwise known as Operation Ostrich.

She'd been right about his relationship with Nikolas, though, and that was why he was at this end of the hallway, near the damaged mural. Man, what a mess. The water had really done a job on it, reducing scenes from the Trojan War and *The Odyssey* to streaks of running color and puckered drywall. The carpet, meanwhile, was still soaked and probably incubating some lethal form of mold.

He sighed. Problems for another day.

He gave the boy's bedroom door a hard knock so he'd be heard against the ear-damaging thump of bass coming from the sound system.

It was Jay-Z again; the hard-core stuff.

Every now and then, Sandro thought about bursting the kid's subversive bubble and telling him that he and his men had listened to Jay-Z all the time in Afghanistan, and Sandro therefore knew many of the words to most of his songs, but he just couldn't do it. He didn't want to disillusion the kid like that. Didn't all teenage boys need to believe that their dads were the biggest dorks in the world?

"Who is it?" Nikolas called.

"Your father," Sandro said, eyeing the collection of signs on the door. This kid was a regular welcome wagon. Caution: Radiation Area said one; Warning: Zombies Ahead said another. Then there was the obligatory red Stop sign, one that said No Trespassing! Violators Will be Shot. Survivors Will be Shot Again, and Sandro's personal favorite: If the Music's Too Loud, You're Too Old.

"Ah...hang on," Nikolas said after a long (and probably horrified) pause.

Then came sudden silence, the thud of a body hitting the floor, and the muffled thunder of large feet moving across a rug.

The door swung open, and there stood Nikolas, looking simultaneously guilty and defiant. His chin was stuck out at that stubborn angle he did so well, but his shoulders were hunched in, as though he expected a beating and was prepared to duck and run if the situation degenerated.

"Aah," Sandro began parsing his words.

One of the problems in dealing with Nikolas was that Sandro could never get the words that came out of his mouth to match his intentions. For example, he might be thinking, *Wow, Nikolas got a good grade on that trigonometry exam,* but what came out of his mouth was, "Why don't you study harder so you can get *A*s in all your classes?"

Every conversation, no matter how trivial, turned into a minefield, and, unfortunately, Sandro hadn't seen a mine-sniffing dog since he returned stateside. Nor did he have any measurable skills in dealing with kids, especially his kid. His supply of patience was far too depleted.

Still, every conversation was a new chance, and Skylar had faith in his ability to become a good father, and her faith seemed important and auspicious. And he desperately wanted to heal this tattered relationship with his son.

So he opened his mouth, treading carefully. "I, aah, just wanted to tell you something."

Uh-oh. Even that was wrong. See? There Nikolas went, crossing his arms over his chest and narrowing his eyes, gestures that were the body-language equivalent of pulling out a pistol and clicking off the safety.

"I did clean my room, okay?" Nikolas snapped. "And I can fold my clothes and put them away later. It's no big deal."

Sandro tilted his head a little, peering over Nikolas's shoulder into the pit in question, which looked pretty much the same as it had the other day, when Sandro had issued the *clean your room or else* edict.

Shoes were still strewn over the floor, textbooks were still piled on the desk, the laundry basket was still mounded with three tons of clean clothes, and the bed was still unmade.

No, wait. The pillows were up off the floor and on the bed now, and the comforter, though still rumpled, had been flapped once or twice so that it covered up most of the white sheets.

It was cleaner, but nowhere near clean.

Sandro thought back on all the terrifying dorm inspections he'd endured during his tenure at West Point and bit back several potential sarcastic replies, choosing to focus on the task at hand.

Connect with your son, Davies.

Anyway, the kid had attempted to make the bed, and there were fewer pairs of shoes on the floor. That was progress, right?

"Yeah, I, aah, see that," Sandro said. "Good job. And there's, aah, no rush on the clothes."

Nikolas's jaw dropped.

"But that's not why I came," Sandro continued. "I just wanted to, aah, mention that you really helped with the yard cleanup. We couldn't've done it without you. So, I, aah…thanks."

Nikolas gaped at him.

Sandro waited, just in case there might be some reply.

Nikolas continued gaping.

O-kay, then.

Well, silence was better than a furious rant, right? And

any conversation that ended without a furious rant was a complete victory, right? Right.

Time to exit the battlefield.

"So." Buoyed by this step in the right direction, the first they'd had in months, possibly years, Sandro clapped the boy on the shoulder and strode off before the fragile peace collapsed. "I'll see you later."

A few minutes later, Sandro braced his palms on the granite counter, leaning into his rising frustration with enough force to move the entire kitchen six inches closer to the beach. His shoulders bunched; his gut churned; his jaw flexed. The flow of his blood had changed into a thrum so loud that it drowned out any other sound that he might hear.

Skylar...Skylar...Skylar...

The sky outside was darkening. So was his mood. The thrill he'd felt at having an argument-free conversation with his son was long gone. Worse, his tenuous grip on sanity was slipping, inch by inch, breaking him into two separate but distinct men.

The one who wished Skylar gone forever and the one who looked for her when she was out of sight.

The one who wanted to do the right thing and the one who could no longer recognize the right thing.

The one who hated Skylar and the one who...

Don't go there, man, he warned himself, tightening his grip on the counter until the muscles in his fingers screamed in protest. *Don't look at her.*

Naturally, he looked. Again.

Raising his head, he stared out the window. She'd made progress in the last couple minutes and was now at the far end of the pool, swinging along on those crutches like a pro, probably heading for the boardwalk where she could watch the sunset.

He watched her, paralyzed by the needs she'd awakened inside him.

He needed her spread-eagled beneath him in bed, her body his for the touching, licking and taking. He needed the thrust of her tongue deep in his mouth and the hot pulse of her slick sex milking him dry. He needed to see her eyes cloud with passion and then, when she was spent, he needed her limp and sweaty body draped over his.

And then he needed it all again. And again and again, until infinity met the horizon, and, more than that, he needed her laughter in his ears, her light in his house and her warmth in his icy heart.

And what about Tony? asked the insidious little voice in the back of his mind that refused to grant him a moment's peace. *What about the man who'd died loving Skylar?*

What about poor dead Tony, your twin brother, you bastard?

Tony? came the answer. *Forget him. Screw him.*

Anyway, wasn't he in Heaven with God? Wasn't he therefore far beyond any petty cares about who was getting with whom down here on earth?

Those were pretty good points, yeah, but the accusatory voice wasn't done with him yet.

What about your honor? it wondered now. *Don't you have any left?*

Hell, those weren't even the right questions. It all boiled down to this: *What do you want more, Sandro?*

The tattered remnants of your honor, or Skylar?

Right now, he wasn't sure he could even scrape together a rudimentary definition of honor. Why was honor so important at this late stage of the game, anyway? Hadn't he lost some when men in his command got killed, then more when he lived but his brother died and then more again when the army shipped him home with a medal and a polite discharge because it couldn't use him after he'd been injured?

Why not forget about honor altogether?

Maybe then he could finally be happy.

"You should go talk to her, Cap."

Startled, Sandro wheeled around to discover Mickey in the kitchen with him, sitting right there, his expression filled with the kind of quiet compassion that didn't do Sandro's aching heart a damn bit of good.

Embarrassed, Sandro cleared his throat, straightened, reached for a glass from the dish rack and filled it, pretending that all he'd been longing for was a glass of water.

"I don't know what you're talking about."

"Sure you do."

Sandro didn't trust his voice, so he shook his head

and raised the glass to his mouth with an unsteady hand, trying to drink.

"Tony's dead, Cap," Mickey said.

"I'd noticed."

"We're coming up on a year he's been gone."

"Do you think I need the reminder?" Sandro snapped.

But Mickey wasn't finished with him yet. "You're alive. She's alive."

Sandro could barely get the words out. "Is there a point to this?"

"Tony would want you to be happy, Cap."

"The question is whether he'd want us to be happy *together,* Mick."

To his pained astonishment, Mickey reached out, caught Sandro's wrist in a hard but comforting grip, and squeezed.

"There's no shame in living, Cap."

With a snarl, Sandro yanked his arm free, not ready to forgive himself or to accept forgiveness if it was offered. It was too damn hard, and he was too damn unworthy.

"Bullshit, Mick," he said quietly. *"Bullshit."*

Sandro couldn't stay away from her, of course.

Wasn't that a foregone conclusion?

The sun was sitting on the horizon by the time he caught up with her on the boardwalk. The sunset was an impressive ambassador for the beauty of this stretch of beach, the glittering gray ocean and his home.

Even so, she was the most spectacular thing in sight, by far—so beautiful that just looking at her sanded the rough edges off his sullen mood. The breeze blew strands of her hair across her high cheekbones, making the ends brush her smiling lips, and the golden light hit her at just the right angle, making her external glow almost as stunning as the one inside her.

"Hi," she said, her gaze focused on the waves.

On his way out the door, he'd paused long enough to grab the living-room throw, and he wrapped it around her shoulders now, over her jacket, because the air was cool and she was precious.

"Are you trying to catch pneumonia on top of everything else?" he grumbled.

He'd expected a lecture about her not being an invalid, and so on and so forth, but she merely caught the edges of the throw and pulled them tighter.

"Thanks."

It took him too long to answer, probably because he was riveted by an unwelcome idea. What if he slipped under that blanket with her, and they stood here together, warm in each other's arms, watching the sunset?

What would that be like? Heaven? Heaven squared?

He cleared his hoarse throat. "You're welcome."

"So I've been wondering," she said after a while. He thought she was going to mention her assertion earlier that he didn't want her to leave, but something else was on her mind. "What do you do now that you're out of the army?"

"Good question," he said darkly. "Know anyone who's hiring?"

After a sidelong grin at him, her gaze reverted to the sunset. "I figured you needed time to recover from your injuries and get settled with Nikolas, right?"

He nodded.

"And you've got the auction house in New York, but I don't figure you for the antiques type."

"You think I'm too uncouth?"

"No. I think you're too restless. So I was thinking maybe you'd do some work as a civilian. Consulting or some such. I understand a lot of retired officers do that sort of thing."

Wow. Was she prescient, or what? "I've had a couple of offers. We'll see."

"And you're good with languages, right?"

"I can get by with a couple, yeah."

She aimed a derisive snort at him. "Oh, a couple. Since your name is Greek and your mother was a Greek professor, I'm guessing you can—" she made quotation marks with her fingers "—*get by* in Greek, right? Say something."

"Ti na po, i kardiá mou?" What should I say, my heart?

Her eyes narrowed with suspicion. "You didn't curse me, did you?"

"No," he said, laughing.

"What else do you speak?"

He stared at her. *"Je parle français, mon ange."* I speak French, my angel.

The uncontrollable tenderness in his voice must have

tipped her off, because she stilled and her breath hitched, and even in the near darkness he thought he could see the color rise in her cheeks.

"What does *mon ange* mean?"

Like he was telling. He studied the horizon, shrugging. "You don't speak French? That's a shame."

Apparently she knew a stone wall when she saw one, because she frowned with suspicion. "Well, anyway, I'm sure you'll have plenty of opportunities. When the time comes."

He had opportunities now, but he felt uncomfortable telling her. How did you mention that the Pentagon needed analysts with your skills without sounding like a pompous ass?

"When the time comes," he agreed instead. "Right now I need to focus on Nikolas."

"He's having problems in school, right?"

This was a moment for a decision. A line he shouldn't cross. Things were getting personal here, and he should slam on the breaks, hit reverse and hightail it back to the house—without her—before they shared any more intimacies. They had already learned way too much about each other.

And yet, he could no more walk away from her now than he could reach past the horizon and hang the sun back in the sky.

"He's having problems adjusting to me being back and the primary parent," he admitted. "And his mother relocating to San Francisco, which was a move he didn't want to make because of his friends. And being a teenage boy. And all of that trickles over into his schoolwork, so, yeah. He's having problems in school."

"Do you...speak to her often? His mother?"

Her tone was light and casual, but she fidgeted a little, twiddling with her earring. He felt a shameful but delicious swoop of delight at her interest in his personal life. Was she jealous?

"Only about Nikolas," he told her.

"You don't miss her?"

He hesitated, because the end of a marriage that had lasted fifteen years required a little thought, and he didn't want to sound like a callous bastard. On the other hand, his overseas deployments had strained a relationship that was never as rock solid as it should have been, and a military marriage was always tricky, especially when both parties had a career. And they'd been divorced for several years.

"No. I don't miss her."

That seemed to satisfy Skylar. For now, at least.

She nodded and stared up at the sky, watching a pelican dive for fish just off the shoreline.

He stared at her.

"How did you stand it?" she asked at last. Her gaze swept down the beach now, encompassing every dune and grass, every tiny crab that might scuttle across her line of sight. "When you were in Afghanistan, how could you stand to be so far away from here? I think I would've taken a vial of sand with me or something."

Ah, man, he thought, looking up to the cloud-scattered sky for help. How was he supposed to manage his feelings when she never gave him a second to catch his breath? When would this woman stop reaching inside him and touching his soul?

"I did take sand with me." Among other precious mementos from home, but he couldn't tell her that.

Her mouth curved in that gentle smile of hers, as though nothing he said surprised her because she knew him so much better than he knew himself.

"Did that help get you through?"

"A lot of things helped me get through."

Now, for the first time, she looked at him, and there was no room in her searching expression for a smile. She was all sweet vulnerability now, with the same sort of urgency he felt every time he looked at her.

He waited, his breath coming short, knowing both that this was another decision point and that he'd make the wrong choice—the one that led him closer to her.

Her voice was a whisper barely audible over the waves. "Did you ever think of me?"

It wasn't that he didn't want to lie; it was that he couldn't.

Not here. Not now. Never with her.

"Yes."

She hesitated. In the pause, he felt her gathering the courage to press her advantage, because she had to know—it had to be written all over his face—that he couldn't deny her anything right now.

"Did you ever think about coming home to me?"

Don't answer that, Davies. Don't answer, don't—

Every day. Every minute. Every second.

"Yes."

She edged closer, her eyes taking up his entire field of vision and forcing the sunset and the ocean to drop away because they were insignificant.

"Were you ever going to do anything about it?"

"It's not that easy."

"It could be."

"Not for me, Sky."

"Why not?"

The want and the frustration both swelled in his chest, making the words hard to find and almost impossible to get out. "Because I'm a single dad. Because I'm trying to find my way back to my son. Because I'm a useless former soldier with no job. Because you're my brother's woman."

"Sandro," she said gently, "your brother's dead."

"I get that, okay? He got killed in the war and I didn't. That guilt is hard enough. How do you expect me to look myself in the mirror knowing I'm alive *and* I'm touching his woman?"

"Please—"

"Huh? You got that figured out?"

Tears made her eyes shimmer in the dying light. "Have you figured out how we're going to say goodbye to each other?"

As if he could. The mere thought of her departure created a black hole so enormous he couldn't see his way around it. She had to know that. She had to know how unhappy this situation made him.

He shook his head, unable to answer.

"Sandro, please—"

"Don't."

"I'm desperate," she said helplessly. "I'll do anything."

His heartbeat screeched to a stop, but there was more, and it was worse.

Without warning, she dropped the ends of the throw and cupped his jaws in her gentle hands, pressing that amazing body all up against his.

He made a strangled sound, agonized by the firm swell of her breasts against his chest, the stroke of her thumbs across his lips and the husky urgency in her voice.

"Did you ever think that you're not the only one who feels guilty, Sandro? Did you ever wonder why I agreed to marry him in the first place, and why I broke up with him? Did you?"

Yeah, he'd wondered, but right now the only questions in his mind were how her mouth tasted and how it'd feel to be buried to the hilt inside her with her legs locked around his waist.

She did that to him. Made him forget what was important.

His face twisted with the excruciating effort of exercising self-control. He couldn't roar with frustration, and he couldn't take her into his arms and kiss her senseless.

Everything was trapped inside him, crowding him, and he couldn't figure out how to break free.

Where did that leave him? Probably well on the road to insanity.

"I don't need to know the answers to those questions," he said roughly. "I don't want to know." Grabbing her wrists, he yanked down her hands and tried not to see the hurt welling in her eyes. "If you feel guilty, too, then you get what I've been saying. You get why we can't do this."

"No," she cried. "You're the problem here, not me! Why can't you understand that something amazing can come out of this complicated situation?"

He looked away, trying to get his heaving lungs under control.

"I'm not giving up on you," she warned.

Chapter 10

Tears prickled the backs of Skylar's eyes as she hobbled back toward the house, and they were the worst kind: hot and bitter, with a whole lot of anger thrown in. She didn't waste time being angry with Sandro, though. Why bother? He hadn't done anything other than be himself and display the sense of honor that she apparently lacked. She couldn't very well fault him for being the kind of man who attracted her so strongly in the first place.

No. Despite what she'd told him, she was the problem here, not him. She was the one who'd saddled up and left Boston to come here, armed only with the lies that she could never quite believe—that her reasons for wanting to see him again weren't personal. That she needed to give him the paperwork relinquishing her share of the estate. That she needed closure. That she needed to make sure he didn't blame her for Tony's death.

All of it was wall-to-wall lies.

Oh, she'd given it her best, sure. Who didn't embrace a little self-delusion from time to time? But the denial was played out, and she'd never been that good at it anyway.

Now was the time to face facts, whether she wanted to or not.

She'd come here because she needed to see Sandro again and determine, once and for all, whether she'd imagined or exaggerated the connection they'd felt the night Tony had introduced them. She'd needed to yank Sandro out from under her skin one way or the other, expel his face from her thoughts and rinse away the longing for him that thrummed in her blood.

How hard could it be, right? What man, upon closer examination, was that fascinating? Surely spending a little more time with him would be the psychological equivalent of roach spray: he'd act like an idiot, maybe, or reveal himself to be a complete jerk, her bubble would burst, she'd get him out of her system and she'd return home to Boston free of his haunting shadow once and for all.

Except that that was more bullshit, wasn't it, Skylar?

Bullshit at a deeper, subtler level, true, but still bullshit.

There was only one truth here, and she'd known it since the night she had arrived.

She was in love with him.

Utterly, desperately and unhappily in love with him.

It didn't make much sense, and it wasn't neat and pretty, but there didn't seem to be anything she could do about it. If she had any success diverting her feelings, Lord knew she wouldn't be here in the Hamptons right now.

What was it about him that touched her so deeply? Was it his quiet strength? His sense of humor? His streak of tenderness that he tried so hard to hide?

She stumbled down the boardwalk, the escalating wind making her eyes stream harder and her leg ache. Was she actually this stupid? Had she actually told him that she wouldn't give up on him?

Way to surrender the keys to the kingdom, girl. Nice job.

But...

On the beach with him just now... She'd thought... She'd seen...

Lust, yeah. Of course. What man alive didn't get turned on when a woman threw herself at him?

Those flashing eyes hid more than desire, though. She'd stake her life on it. She'd seen his longing, felt his stark loneliness and sensed his desperation.

Not that any of that mattered.

That was the kicker. Maybe he did love her. Maybe, in another life, they'd already be well on their way to living happily ever after and making babies. Unfortunately, in this life, Sandro's moral code wouldn't allow him to touch her, and that was the only thing that mattered.

Her biggest fear was that she could talk, plead or beg until her tongue shriveled up and died from overuse, and he would listen to her. He might even yearn for her. But would he ever change his mind?

God. What if he never changed his mind?

Swiping at her wet face, she cleared the swaying grasses and headed for the house, which loomed in front of her in the darkness.

Except that it wasn't entirely dark. Bright yellow light blazed in several of the windows. She frowned, wondering what was wrong with this picture, and then it hit her: the power was back on.

The realization set off another wave of hopelessness, which was just the thing she needed. Even in her advanced state of denial, she couldn't fool herself about the significance of the power being back on.

Today, the power was back on, and tomorrow, for certain, the road would be clear. There would be no more delays.

As if that wasn't bad enough, she was the genius who'd volunteered to cook dinner tonight. Brilliant.

"There you are, Skylar." Just ahead, the shadows shifted and Nikolas emerged on the path cradling something against his chest. The croon of his voice was nearly drowned out by a series of high-pitched mewls. "Guess what I've got here?"

"Oh!"

Reaching out, she took one of the squirming kittens by its scruff and put her other hand under its bottom. This cute little bag of bones and fur was exactly what she needed to pull herself out of the despair she'd been headed for.

She rubbed her cheek against the soft little white patch on his black forehead, grateful to have something accept her love, even if it couldn't be Sandro. The kitten nuzzled happily, and she felt the rough swipe of its tongue.

"Aren't you precious?" she cooed.

"The tuna worked," Nikolas said. "They were out here inhaling it."

"Good job." Rearranging the kitten so that she had a free hand, she gave Nikolas a high five. "Let's get these little guys in the house so I can check them out and make sure they're healthy."

Taking his elbow, she resumed her slow hobble up the path, but he stopped, a worried crease developing between his brows.

"Ah," he began.

"What?"

"Dad's not going to be happy about more animals in the house," he said grimly. "We might be putting our lives at risk."

Since she'd had more than enough of the high-and-mighty Sandro and the lengthy list of the things he would or wouldn't allow, she didn't bother keeping the sarcasm out of her voice.

"Oh, really?"

She thought of the kittens, which needed shelter. She thought of her heart, which was hurting, perhaps broken. She thought of Sandro and his cool-eyed gaze and reinforced walls designed to keep her out. Most of all, she thought of the hints of passion she'd seen beneath his surface layer of ice.

Maybe she'd never change his mind, but she could damn sure be a thorn in his side every second of every minute until she went home. Hell, at this point, she felt like she was entitled to whatever perverse pleasure she could get.

"You leave your father to me, Nikolas."

After she left, Sandro spent a good hour or more on the dark beach with his face to the wind, the better to feel the icy prickle of the ocean's spray. The pound of the surf did not provide peace. The salty air did not clear his mind. Even when his entire frame had turned to a block of ice, he felt no relief from the heat of his frustrated longing for Skylar, a woman he couldn't (or was it *wouldn't?*) give himself permission to have.

His body felt tight-wired and frayed, like elevator cables that could no longer support an overloaded car and had begun to unravel. His heart was a boulder inside his chest and its beat was a dull thud.

Never in his life had he been this lost. If he'd been dropped into an Amazonian rain forest at midnight, armed with only a compass, a flashlight and a granola bar, he'd have an easier time figuring things out than he did now.

Eventually, it occurred to him that, appealing as the idea might be, he couldn't spend the night on the beach. So, in a fog of his own making, he trudged back to the house, slipped into the kitchen, and confronted a Norman Rockwell-ian scene that further tilted his earth on its axis.

This isn't my house, he thought.

His house was cold, dark and empty, even when the power was up and running. *His* house was indifferent to its inhabitants, gathering dust and gloom wherever it could and blocking any light or life that may want to seep in through the windows. *His* house smelled of emptiness and neglect, except when the occasional scorch of burned microwave popcorn livened things up a bit.

This was no longer that house.

This house was alive with a blaze of overhead lights, the flicker of candles on the table and the crackle of a fire in the hearth. This house had toasty warmth and the inviting smells of well-cooked steaks and something chocolaty to draw him closer. People were allowed to be relaxed and cheerful in this house, as evidenced by the laughing faces of Skylar as she stirred something on the stove and Mickey as he jabbed at the logs with the brass poker and Nikolas as he thumped out an upbeat African rhythm on his drum.

Sandro stared, riveted with disbelief.

Three goblets filled with red wine sat on the table, which meant that drinking could now be done for pleasure here, as a social activity rather than as the furtive and desperate attempts of a man to wash bitter memories out of his head.

Food was plentiful for once, and he saw broccoli, yeast rolls, baked potatoes and some kind of nibbly appetizer—were those *cheese straws?*—laid out for their enjoyment.

Even the damn bird was happy, chattering and bobbing along his perch atop the mantel.

And then, as though they'd all been zapped with some invisible signal, they saw Sandro, gave a nasty start and froze, looking caught and guilty. Clearly, any feelings of joy could not survive for long in Sandro's presence; the party, as far as they were concerned, was now over.

Sandro also froze.

He had the humbling and unwelcome thought that if the three of them had a choice between sharing their dinner with him or with a group of terrorist extremists, they'd take the terrorists, no question.

Abrupt silence engulfed the kitchen.

Sandro's coiled nerves unraveled a bit more, because he just couldn't get his world figured out. The whole time he was in Afghanistan, he'd dreamed of coming home. Lived for it. And for what? So he could brood, wallow in his survivor's guilt and bring gloom with him wherever he went? So he could turn away from a woman so amazing she made the breath catch in his throat? So his son could flinch when he saw him walk into the room?

Was that what he wanted from his life? Or was…*this?*

Could it be as simple as making a choice?

Could he make it?

How, in just a few short days, had Skylar been able to pry open his eyes and show him what he was missing? What additional vistas could she open up for him if he let her? What could his life be like if she was in it?

His head spun with the questions…and the possibilities.

"Sandro." Skylar, predictably, recovered first, jarring him out of his thoughts. With one hand on the counter for support, she edged closer and offered him one of the goblets of wine. "You're just in time."

Trapped behind the wall of his emotions, the one he could never quite climb, he could barely speak.

"What's going on here?"

Her chin was tipped up, her eyes bright with defiance. "We're celebrating the power being back on. Don't you want some wine?"

He stared at her.

She shrugged. "Oh, well. Your choice. Cheers."

Toasting him, she drank. Around the glass's rim he could see the way her lips quirked with unmistakable triumph, as though his discomfiture strengthened her.

Damn, he supposed it did.

Before anyone could say anything else, something brushed against his ankle, making him jump.

"What the hell?"

"Careful," Skylar warned, stooping down to scoop up the offender. "It's one of the kittens."

"Excuse me?"

She straightened with a squirming black ball of fur and whiskers pressed to her cheek and made the introductions, as though they were at some delightful cocktail party.

"This one's the male. Luke. That one over there—" she pointed toward the fireplace, where another fur ball had his paws pressed against the bricks and was meowing hopefully up at the bird "—is Leia."

"No C-3PO?"

Another careless shrug from Skylar. "There could be. There's no telling how big their litter was. These are the only ones we've found so far."

"What are they doing here?"

Skylar's eyes, like the kitten's, were a study in innocence. "We knew you wouldn't want them out in the cold without their mother. Poor little things."

Pausing only to shoot glares at Nikolas and Mickey, who were both doing a lousy job of trying not to grin, he focused all of his growing fury on Skylar. She was the problem here.

"I thought I told you I didn't want animals in this house."

"Oh, I know," she agreed. "So we're only keeping them for a few days. Until we can get them to a shelter. Unless you fall in love with them, of course."

That unlikely image set off a wave of sniggering from the peanut gallery.

Sandro ignored it, all of his attention irrevocably centered on Skylar.

Dropping his voice, he spoke only to her. He had to defend his position because he'd been a soldier and that was what soldiers were trained to do.

To fight. Hold the line. Win.

"You'll be gone in a few days."

That gleam of amusement in her eyes intensified, and he had the galling idea that she felt sorry for him.

"Gone, maybe," she told him. "But never forgotten."

This undeniable truth sent him stalking from the kitchen and down the hall, into his den, where he slammed the door against her, as though that would do any good.

At eleven forty-three that night, when the house was quiet and Skylar couldn't twiddle her thumbs in her room for another minute—waiting for sleep to take her when she knew it would never come—she went looking for Sandro.

Anger propelled her, blocking out the ache in her leg.

She was stupid for throwing herself at a man who kept rejecting her, but he was a fool for not seeing what was right in front of him. The two of them had a genuine connection, the kind that people could spend their lives yearning for, and he couldn't throw it away fast enough.

And for what? Something concrete? No. It was all because of his misplaced guilt and misguided sense of honor. And did he care how it ripped her guts out, dooming her to a life spent wondering about what could have been if the stars had aligned differently? No. He'd bar-

ricaded himself so deep inside his little cave of martyr-
dom that he couldn't see the effect he was having on her.

That was about to change, though.

She was sick of him. Sick of his roadblocks. Sick with
longing.

And he was going to hear about it.

The gloom in the first-floor hallway was an eerie reminder of the night she had arrived. Once again, the only
illumination came from a sliver of yellow light through
the cracked study door, and she had that same feeling of
foreboding, because when a woman confronted a lion in
his den, she was likely to get bitten, if not mauled.

She banged through the door, anyway, not caring if
she disturbed him. Wanting to disturb him.

He sat behind the desk, as though he'd been waiting
for her, his face half in shadow because the light from the
corner lamp only reached so far. An unmoving, hulking
presence, he had his elbows planted on the desk, his fingers woven together, and his mouth pressed against the
fisted mass of his hands. Surliness seemed to have swallowed his face, leaving only the heavy line of his brows
slashed low over the gleam of his eyes.

A glass filled with two fingers of scotch sat, un-
touched, on the desk in front of him.

Their gazes caught and held.

In a calculated move, she'd come down dressed only
in her nightgown, that virginal cotton number that revealed more than it covered. She could feel the slow glide
of his gaze as it skimmed over the neck's low scoop…

the thrust of her engorged nipples…the wide curve of her hips…the columns of her bare legs…the dark triangle at their apex.

In the dangerous silence, she heard the catch of his breath, and that gave her enough courage to approach him. Leaning against the end of the desk, she hooked a knee around the corner and eased herself into a sitting position on top of the desk, making sure that her hem slipped up to her thighs.

His turbulent gaze skimmed over this newly revealed flesh and then flickered up to her face, still and waiting.

"I want you to know what you missed," she said.

One dark brow arched.

"While you were in here hiding, or sulking, or whatever it is that you do when life goes on around you, we were having a great time eating dinner together in the kitchen."

"Is that so?"

The distinct note of boredom in his low voice didn't fool her for a minute. They were close to a breakthrough, she and Sandro; the feeling was so strong she could almost stick out her tongue and taste it.

"We had rare steaks and fresh bread. Your son made chocolate-chip cookies because he likes to cook. You probably didn't know that about him."

A rumble, something like a warning growl, vibrated in his throat.

"We talked for a long time. Mickey told us about his adventures in basic training. Nikolas told us about getting kicked out of his camp last summer. It was for fighting, but did you know why he was fighting?"

Sandro said nothing.

"It's because he was sticking up for this other kid who got bullied, which I think is pretty cool. Not the fighting part—the courage that it took for your son to stand up to his peers. That's really something. But then we played a few rounds of poker, and Nikolas cheated. Twice. So I'd say you've got some work to do on that front. He loves animals, too. Did you know that? Asked me lots of questions about being a vet and my practice. I like him. A lot. He's a great kid. And Mickey's a great friend to you."

"I live for your opinion."

"I figured you'd want to know."

"And that's why you paraded all the way down here in your thin little nightgown, giving yourself a chill?" He shot a significant glance at her beaded nipples, which had to be clearly visible beneath the filmy cups of cotton. "To tell me what I missed at dinner?"

She smiled her most predatory smile. "That's part of it, yeah."

"And what's the rest, pray tell?"

Planting her palms on the desk, she leaned forward, into his face, hunching her shoulders like Marilyn Monroe and causing her gaping gown to reveal more of her breasts. He noticed. That fathomless black gaze dipped, lingered and then flickered back to her face.

He looked murderous now.

"I want you to know that I'm a great woman, and I'm crazy about you. I think about you all the time—"

"Think about me?" he echoed, his voice nearly inaudible now.

"I think about everything you've said and done, and everything I wish I knew about you and everything I wish we could do together. I think about the night we met and the connection we—yes, *we,* don't deny it—felt for each other. And here's what I really wanted to say."

"Don't keep me in suspense."

"If you let me go, you will regret it."

He paused, nostrils flaring. "Are you a mind reader now?"

"Deny it, then."

Something forced him to open his mouth but he closed it again, floundering.

"You'll regret it," she repeated. "You'll think about how you missed the chance to come up to my bedroom and make love to me. You'll never know how hot I am for you or how wet I get when you look at me—"

His gleaming gaze wavered and fell. He shifted in his chair, lips tightening.

"—and you'll never know what it feels like to be inside me or if I'll scratch your back when I come. Maybe I love it from behind, hard and rough—"

He made a choked sound.

"—but you'll never know, will you? And I'm going to feel sorry for you. Because when I go back to Boston, I'll know that I did my very best. I did everything humanly possible to explore a relationship with you and see if this chemistry between us is as special as I think it is. But all you'll have is regret that you blew it."

Utterly still now, he stared off at the far wall with unfocused eyes. If she had to guess, she'd say he wasn't even breathing, and she knew she'd finally hit a nerve.

Pressing her advantage, she leaned forward a bit more, just enough to brush her lips against his ear as she whispered to him. "Sleep well."

Undone, Sandro watched her go, taking with her the glow of her bare skin, her brain-fogging fragrance of fruity shampoo and the promise of ecstasy in her eyes.

Only his fear of being overheard kept him from swiping everything off his desk and roaring out his frustration like a rampaging Godzilla.

He couldn't think.

His pounding head felt like it might explode, which would at least disperse the seething images of him thrusting hard and deep into Skylar's sweat-slicked body. On the other hand, maybe if he squeezed hard enough he could crush his skull between his palms, blocking out Skylar's taunting voice that way. Yes. Good idea. He pressed his temples until sparks of white light marred his vision and his lips pulled back in a gargoyle's grimace, but it didn't help.

Everywhere he looked, Skylar was there.

Agitation got him up on his feet and sent him pacing in front of the fire.

He thought of the racking emptiness inside him and

the fact that it didn't have to be that way if he chose— and he saw now that it was a choice—to rejoin the living.

He thought of Skylar's warmth.

He thought of his house with and without her, which was the difference between Disneyland and a crypt.

Most of all, he thought of Tony, his missing other half.

Striding to the mantel, he tipped up his face to Tony's graduation picture, but found he could barely look at it because of the blinding guilt and anger. He was alive; Tony was dead. Why had Tony died and left him here alone? *Why?* He had a whole life ahead of him; Tony didn't. Tony had claimed Skylar first, and for that, Sandro had hated him. It wasn't right, but he had. Sandro could be with Skylar right now; Tony, even if he were still alive, never could.

Was any of that fair?

Was fairness even the issue?

Or was the issue, simply, that life was for the living?

He couldn't decide.

And then he thought about his desire to honor Tony's life by staying away from Skylar, and about his uncontrollable desire for Skylar.

He put the two desires on a scale, weighing them against each other.

It wasn't even close.

Wouldn't Tony understand? Wouldn't he want the people he'd loved to be happy, even if they were happy together? Hadn't he been that kind of person?

The decision came over Sandro, filling him with a new calm.

This time, he had no problems looking into Tony's earnest young face as it stared back at him from the photo.

"Please understand, man," he said. "I didn't mean for it to happen, but I have to do this. I can't let her go. So I have to let you go."

Tony's brown eyes were so vivid and familiar, so piercing, that Sandro felt his brother as an actual presence in the room with him. So it was a vague disappointment when Tony didn't move inside his frame and say something, like a magical photo.

Sandro waited another beat or two, just to be sure, but the only response he got was the swelling peace inside his chest.

It was enough.

Kissing the tips of his first two fingers, he pressed the kiss to Tony's forehead and rubbed it in.

"You're my brother. I'll never forget you. I love you, man."

And then he turned his back on both the photo and the past, and went upstairs, to Skylar.

Chapter 11

Skylar's room was at the far end of the hallway, well away from the others, and he slipped into it quietly, not bothering to knock. He didn't see her at first, but then she materialized as a lonely figure on the balcony, her palms braced on the rail. One of the French doors was cracked open enough to let in a hint of the cool breeze, but not enough to chill the room. The sheer curtains fluttered a little, as did the hem of her nightgown. Moonlight lined her troubled face as she stared down at the ocean's dark glitter, and he made himself a silent promise on the spot: if he had to make it his life's work, he'd never put that look on her face again.

Crossing the room, he edged through the French door and out on the balcony behind her, opening his mouth to call her name. He didn't need to. She sensed his presence and glanced at him over her shoulder, revealing tear-streaked cheeks that nearly tore him in half. At the sight of him, her face twisted with a tortured combination of joy and relief.

"Don't." He kept approaching and stopped only when he'd pulled her into his arms and pressed the length of his body against the back of hers. She was pliant and eager, and her hand came up to caress his face as he kissed and nuzzled her cheek. "Don't cry, okay? Don't cry."

"I was afraid you wouldn't come," she whispered against his mouth.

He held her tighter, letting one of his hands drift down to the soft curve of her belly. He was hungry for the feel of her and he couldn't control his hands any more than he could control the slow thrust of his hips against her. His erection was already full and insistent, and it fit perfectly in the groove between the two halves of her tight butt.

"Even I'm not that stupid," he told her.

She laughed. He stared at the mouth he'd never kissed and swallowed hard. She lifted her chin and twisted her neck just a little bit farther, enough so that she could look him in the eye as she gave him the most precious gift imaginable.

"I love you," she said. "You have no idea how much I love you."

That was it. Overcome, he caught her face in his hand and kissed her. Her mouth was slick and minty, her tongue eager. She opened for him, mewling with pleasure, and he marveled at all the infinite ways their lips could fit together.

Soon the sucking turned to nipping, the nipping to biting, and before he knew it, he was filling his hands with her soft breasts and shaking with urgency.

Breathing was all but impossible.

They broke apart, panting.

Her lips were swollen and wet now, her eyes feverish with need. He knew the feeling. It amazed him that he'd had anything to do with making her burn so hot that her body nearly singed his palms. Sandro couldn't get enough of her.

She paused. Focused. "Please tell me you're not going to regret this tomorrow."

"There's no way in hell."

"And we're going to figure out how to be together, right?"

He stroked her again, rubbing his thumb back and forth over one hard nipple. "We are together. Period."

"No doubts?"

"No doubts. Come inside."

"No. Now. Like this." She pressed her back against the length of his body again.

"So you *do* like it from behind. Duly noted."

"Let's do it here."

Here was the balcony on a moonlit but chilly night, with the ocean breeze in their faces, not that she looked concerned. Still, she'd been injured and he wasn't taking any chances with her health.

"But—"

"*Now,* Sandro."

To sweeten the pot, she reached up under the hem of her nightgown and wriggled out of a pair of dark panties, dropping them to the ground beneath her bare feet. With one hand, she braced herself against the railing, bending at the waist. With the other hand, she kept the hem up around her waist and presented him with the heart-stopping brown plum of her bare ass.

She glanced over her shoulder at him again, her eyes a wild gleam behind her wind-whipped hair. "Now," she said again. "I can't wait."

"You'll wait," he said grimly, his control close to snapping. "I don't want you catching pneumonia. And I want to see your face."

Grabbing her hand, he tugged her inside, nudging the door shut with his foot. She wheeled around, into his arms, and their hungry mouths found their way back to each other. Frantic now, they rubbed and scratched, licked and sucked, trying to find that exact perfect position even though it was already clear that their bodies had been made for this and nothing else.

She was amazing.

He was undone.

Stunned, he broke the kiss so he could look at her and work on catching his breath, but his heaving lungs weren't up to the job. A hint of a smile curled her lips as their gazes connected, and it was a real shame that he couldn't get his voice to work. He had a lot to tell her, and all of it was beautiful.

Jesus, he thought, shaking his head. He couldn't look away.

Inside her sparkling eyes, he saw love and light. A joyful future and—

"What was I thinking?" he wondered.

Her brow quirked. "What?"

"Why did I fight you so hard? Because of my honor? Screw honor."

"Don't say that. That's who you are."

"Honor doesn't make me feel like you do. Thank God you're more stubborn than I am."

"Thank God," she agreed, grinning.

Sandro backed into the nearest chair, sat, and went to work on his belt and the button of his jeans, appalled by both his shaking hands and his need. He had some moves, and she deserved for him to use them. They had a huge fluffy bed, and they could lose themselves in it by simply walking across the room. Down the hall in his medicine cabinet, there were condoms that he should employ.

None of that mattered.

Neither of them needed anything other than this, anyway.

So he freed his straining length from the confines of his boxer briefs with one hand, and tested the soft petals of flesh between her thighs with the fingers on his other. She was slick and swollen and ready for him. More than that, she was responsive to his slightest touch as she straddled him, crooning and arching her back, circling her hips and rubbing herself against him without shame.

And he was lost.

Gripping the curve of her hip to anchor her, he ran the head of his penis back and forth against her.

Ah, yes. She was tight. So tight.

Inch by inch, he moved inside her, surging and easing back, surging a little farther…and a little farther again as she settled her full weight upon him. Shuddering with restraint, he leaned his forehead against hers for a moment's respite—at this rate, he wasn't going to make it—and discovered, as he ran his hands across her back, that the soft barrier of her nightgown infuriated him. Starting tonight, nothing and no one would ever come between them again. So he swept the nightgown up and off, revealing the satiny gleam of her bare shoulders and the perfect swells of her dark tipped breasts, bouncing gently.

That's what he wanted.

He surged again. Easy…easy…*easy*…and—*God*.

Before he knew it, she'd swallowed him up to the base and the blinding pleasure blocked out the rest of the world—except for the sudden emotion that hit him in a blinding wave.

She was so beautiful. So earthy and sexy, with her head tilted back, swollen lips parted and glazed eyes half closed. So freaking incredible that he couldn't get his mind around his good fortune.

And he was so lost in her that nothing could ever be the same again.

The emotions kept coming, choking him up and forcing him to twist up his face in a vain effort to hold it all back.

"What's wrong?" she cooed, nuzzling his cheek with her kisses. "Tell me what's wrong."

"That's it—nothing's wrong."

"Is that bad?"

"Just unexpected. You're a gift. The greatest gift. I hope you know that."

Her mouth found his again, opening wide and her tongue thrusting deep, but not before she murmured in his ear: "I love you, Sandro. I love you."

They found their languid rhythm, and there was only this: their cries in the night, her swiveling hips filling his hands as they moved together, and the indescribably perfect friction of his body sliding within hers.

Their surroundings came slowly back into focus.

She was on the huge bed now, her body stretched across silky white linens. Drowsy and drunk with pleasure, her lips curled in a smile, she stretched her arms toward the headboard, equally aware of the arch of her back and the intensity of his avid gaze on her. All her senses were heightened, and she experienced everything in vivid detail: the cooling sweat between her breasts…

the musky scent of their satisfaction…the sweetly delicious ache between her thighs.

Making love with Sandro had done nothing to quench her desire for him.

If anything, the lust burned hotter than ever inside her.

Propping up on one elbow, she studied him from beneath her heavy lids and reached out to beckon him with her free arm.

"Come here," she murmured.

"In a minute."

"What are you doing?"

"Looking at you."

There was no need to ask if he liked what he saw. He stood by the side of the bed, staring down at her, his eyes bright and his face dark with desire. He'd ditched his shirt at some point, revealing a taut torso with every ridge defined and every hard muscle lovingly carved. Even the scar from his injury intensified his rugged appeal.

A strip of sleek black hair collected between his dark brown nipples, traveling south to where his unbuttoned pants gave way to black boxer briefs. Behind the underwear strained a heavy erection that made her squirm with renewed need.

As she watched, his gaze slid over her body, lingering on her lips, the stiff peaks of her nipples, and the cleft between her thighs.

He went utterly still, except for the slow heave of his rib cage, thinning lips and tightening jaw.

After several beats, his scalding gaze flicked back up to her face.

Her heart slowed to a hard thud, and they stared at each other, neither moving.

"It didn't help, did it?" she asked.

"Making love?" He shook his head. "It made me want you more. I didn't think that was possible."

He didn't exactly look thrilled with this development, which made a shadow flit across her heart.

"You said no regrets," she reminded him.

A lazy smile curled one edge of his mouth. "Oh, I don't regret anything."

The velvet caress of his voice ran over her skin, making her shiver. It might have been wiser to try to hide her rising lust, but there was no way she could manage it. She'd never been able to rein in the way he made her feel, which was unreasonably alive. She had lived perfectly well when she was alone, yeah, but she could only soar when she was with him.

"Touch me, then," she said.

He started with her face, tracing curves and ridges, exploring bone structure. Unraveling, bit by bit, she let her neck lean back, and those long fingers trailed down her throat and paused in the valley between her breasts. This, naturally, made her breath catch and her blood surge until her lips, nipples and sex throbbed with arousal.

The gleam in his eyes was wicked, and she was wicked, too, because there was something vulnerable and illicit about being spread naked before him, and she loved it. Reveled in it.

"Don't stop."

Twisting at the waist, she watched as his dark hand swallowed her paler breast, stroking and massaging until she crooned with pleasure. The contrast between his strong fingers and her soft flesh was unbearably erotic.

And then he reached between her legs.

She cried out, undone by the intimacy.

It was more than the relentless glide of his slick fingers that stunned her. It was the way his gaze latched onto hers and held, demanding that she look at him, and nowhere else, as he drove her to orgasm.

"Sandro," she gasped, writhing against him.

"Don't close your eyes."

Easier said than done. *"Sandro—"*

"I'm wondering, did we make a baby tonight?"

"No."

His expression was unreadable. "No?"

She undulated without shame. There was no time for it. No room for it. Every atom in her body concentrated in that point of contact between them, making it hard for rational thoughts to form.

"I'm on the...on the...on the pill—aah, God."

The wave crested and crashed over her, eased back, and then came again, harder. Propped up on both elbows now, she rode it out with his fingers inside her, prolonging the ecstasy, and his gaze riveted on her face. She had the feeling he was determined to milk every last expression, breath and mewl out of her, until only a shell was left.

She didn't mind a bit.

Nor did she mind when he kept that possessive hand on her engorged nub, marking his place, while he worked on freeing himself from his boxers with the other. She glimpsed his erection for the first time, and she saw, with a dizzying burst of clarity, that it was long and thick, with a plump head that was ruddy with blood.

He crawled over her, nudging her legs apart with one of his knees. She opened her thighs and arms for him, and he settled his weight on her.

"But you like children," he continued, easing inside her again, slowly…carefully…as though he knew how her body stretched to accommodate him and didn't want to hurt her, "don't you?"

"I love children."

The beginnings of a smile crinkled the corners of his eyes as he lowered his head, positioning his mouth until it was a breath away from hers.

"We've got a lot to talk about, Sky."

"Hmm." The conversation stalled as his hips began to swivel. "Later." And then his tongue filled her mouth.

"Go to sleep. Get some rest," Sandro told her. "You're tired."

She was lying on her belly now, stretched out next to him, her head pillowed on her folded arms. Only half of her face was visible, but he only needed that half to see the drowsy warmth in her eyes and the way her cheeks plumped with a slow smile.

"I'm not tired. I'm happy."

He was on his side with his head resting on one palm. With his free hand, he traced circles on her bare back because his skin was hungry for hers and he'd spent way too much time resisting the impulse to touch her.

It was now three-fifteen, and the only illumination came from the weak moonlight filtering past the closed drapes. The night was almost over with little actual sleep having been done, and if Skylar was tired, it was his fault because he was the greedy bastard who couldn't keep his hands off her. Still, she'd been through a lot in the last several days, and he needed to remember that now that she was officially his to protect and treasure.

"You can be tired and happy at the same time," he pointed out. "Go to sleep."

She ignored the directive.

Typical.

"Are you happy?" she wondered.

He damn sure was. What other explanation could there be for the blossoming light inside him, as though he'd swallowed the sun?

"You have no idea."

Her smile widened to a grin just before her eyes drooped closed, and he thought maybe she'd let go enough to drift off, but there was more on her mind.

"What now?" she asked softly.

Several answers were on the tip of his tongue, starting with pressing issues like: *now we figure out how to braid our lives together;* or *now we figure out what to tell Nikolas.* But once he'd opened his mouth, he discovered that there was really only one thing he needed to know, even if the subject—which, by the way, was incompatible with her going to sleep and getting some rest—twisted his gut into a sickening knot.

He thought he was ready to hear it but, on the other hand, he wasn't sure he'd ever be able to understand it.

Still. There was no time like the present.

"Maybe now you could tell me…about Tony."

Her lids flicked open, revealing a worried gleam in her eyes. "Are you sure?"

Was he sure he wanted to hear about how she'd loved his perfect brother before she'd loved him? How, if things had worked out differently, she could now be his sister-in-law instead of his woman? Or maybe he should be the one confessing right now, starting with how his sorrow over his brother's death only took him so far, and if he had the choice of a live brother who might still have a chance with Skylar, or a dead brother but Skylar here, vibrant and alive in his life and in his bed, he wasn't sure which he would choose?

Was he sure he was ready to face any of that? Yeah, sure. Just like a PFC on his first deployment was ready for an exchange of fire with the enemy.

But he was supposed to be the brave type, and he wasn't good with vulnerability, so…

"Yeah," he said.

Nodding, she rolled over and sat up, propping herself on the pillows and pulling the linens to cover her bare body. The gesture hit him hard, like a rejection, which was ridiculous. There was no need to feel like Adam being expelled from the Garden of Eden's sensual beauty, he told himself, but the foreboding stayed with him.

"I volunteered to provide medical care for some of the service dogs," she began. "I met him that way."

That old familiar tension ran up and down his spine, tightening his muscles. "I know. He told me."

"He was handsome. He made me laugh. He flirted—"

Given Tony's way with women—easy and natural, a regular thrill to behold—Sandro could just imagine. The mere idea of his perfect brother charming and seducing Skylar sat on the back of his tongue in a lump, sour and indigestible.

"—and then he came back the next day to ask me out. So I said yes."

All very fascinating, but when would she get to the point?

"You loved him," he said flatly.

She shrugged helplessly. "I was swept up in the excitement of it. And everyone loved Tony—"

There it was. The story of his life with its silent corollary: *Why can't you be more like Tony?* Why should Skylar be different from anyone else he'd ever known, including his parents? Why should this one person prefer Sandro when no one else ever had?

He nodded, sickened by the slow shrivel of his heart.

"—but I didn't love him enough, Sandro. Not the way I should have."

He felt his brain contract, trying to make that sentence work to his benefit, but he couldn't manage it. He was a soldier; linguistic and emotional nuances like that were lost on him, and this subject was too important to let anything get lost in the translation.

"You're going to have to spell that out for me, Sky. I'm not the touchy-feely type."

"It means that I let the relationship go way further than it ever should have."

"What does *that* mean?"

"If you want me to tell you the truth, you probably shouldn't bite my head off."

That settled him down in a hurry. There was something about her quiet reproach that made him feel like a slime-trailing slug. As a sign of how far he'd come in the last several days with her, he gave it to her straight.

To his surprise, it wasn't that hard to get the words out.

"I'm jealous."

She stilled, her eyes widening. "What?"

Peeling back the layers of his soul, he discovered, wasn't so hard when Skylar was the one listening. "Don't get me wrong. I was used to being jealous of Tony. I lived with it every day of my life. Anything I could do, he could do quicker and better. Skateboarding. Grades. Girls. West Point. He was always the example I could never live up to. Do you get that?"

She nodded.

"That was fine. I was used to it. It made me work harder. No problem—"

"Sandro—"

"—until the night I met you and realized he'd already claimed you first. That wasn't okay because I wanted you. I wanted him gone, and it wasn't friendly competition or sibling rivalry. For the first time in my life, I hated my brother. I couldn't look at him. It made me sick, Sky—"

"Shh," she said, reaching for him.

Maybe now wasn't the time for this conversation, after all. Too many things were still raw and fragile, especially their new relationship. And anyway, Tony was gone and they were here, together, and the past couldn't hurt them unless he let it.

He wouldn't let it.

So he peeled the linens down her body and out of his revealing engorged breasts with those dark and jutting nipples, and the labored heave of her rib cage.

Looking at her stopped his heart. Every damn time.

Putting his hands on her hips, he pulled her until flat on her back with her legs hooked around Then he leaned in, kissing her hard and deep took his erection and, with a single thrust of his home.

home for him, and somehow he'd known

Panting now, he laced their fingers together and held them back over her head as he set a frenzied pace that had her face twisting with rapture.

"You belong with me," he told her, breaking the kiss just long enough to stake his claim, once and for all. "You've always belonged with *me*."

"I know," she said.

"I don't see why this couldn't wait till the sun was up," Sandro grumbled.

"Because we were awake anyway, and they're kittens. We'll just check on them, make sure they're okay, and go back to bed for a while."

"Back to bed, did you say?"

Here, Sandro paused on the step below hers, shooting her a grin over his shoulder. It was still dark, with only a console lamp in the foyer to light their way, but light enough for her to see the wicked glint in his eyes.

She, naturally, melted into a puddle of simpers and blushes.

Seeing this, Sandro turned all the way around, pressed his face into the valley between her breasts, where the silky edges of her robe came together, and breathed deep. That was bad enough. But then he slid his lips up and down the sensitive column of her neck, planted his hands on her butt and pulled her closer.

To her credit, she did try to resist.

"Sandro," she gasped, angling her head to give him better access to a sweet spot. "Will you—aah, God. Will you focus, please? Focus! We have animals to check o

With that, she slid her hands up between them and shoved the unforgiving slab of his chest. He backed up, muttering.

"The kittens are fine," he said reasonably. "If anyone needs your attention right now, it's me."

"I am so not impressed."

"And I'm freezing my ass off. The bed is warm."

That made her laugh. "No one told you to come."

He gave her a dark look as he took her hand to lead her on their slow descent to the first floor. "I'm coming. That's the best way to make sure you're quick about it. Plus, your leg is still a little shaky. I don't want you to tumble to your death down the stairs. That would ruin my chances of getting laid again."

"You're such a compassionate lover. You'll have to give me a minute. I'm choked up."

"Smart-ass."

As soon as he hit the bottom, he turned to grab her around the waist. Laughing, he swung her around like a little girl, and their mutual giddiness soon dissolved into a kiss...a sigh...a croon...

"Looks like we interrupted something, man."

The unexpected and unwelcome sound of Mickey's sarcastic voice made them jump as though they'd been zapped by a taser. They broke apart. Sandro set her on her wobbly feet, hanging onto her elbow until she was steady. She turned within the circle of his arms and took a quick swipe at her hair, which felt like an electrified rat's nest. Behind her, Sandro cleared his throat in the gaping silence.

Oh, God.

It was as bad as she'd feared.

Mickey and Nikolas, both still in their pajamas and robes, were right there in the doorway from the living room. Luke sat, mewling, in Mickey's lap, while Nikolas held a squirming Leia against his chest and tried to keep her away from Skywalker, who was perched on his shoulder and glaring down at the kitten with a beady and suspicious eye.

An endless beat passed, during which Skylar was excruciatingly aware of Mickey's amused grin and Nikolas's dropped jaw.

She and Sandro recovered and scrambled for a cover story at the same time.

"We were just checking on the animals—"

"We were thirsty—"

"Well, we were going to have a drink after we fed the animals—"

"And I was a little hungry, too, so we thought a snack might be—"

"Wow," Nikolas said to Sandro. "And you claim I'm a bad liar when I get caught."

Skylar and Sandro shut up and exchanged a furtive glance. She wondered if her hot face was now glowing orange like lava.

Mickey gave them an approving look. "Thank God you two finally got together. You could cut the sexual tension around here with a knife. It was like mating season in the cat house at the zoo—"

"Thank you, Mickey, for that delicate assessment," Sandro cut in, his voice and expression glacial.

"No problem, Cap," Mickey said.

Sandro looked to Nikolas and seemed to struggle with his words. He fidgeted, scrubbing a hand over his head. "Skylar, aah…she means a lot to me, and I, aah…well, I mean that we—"

Nikolas's brows rose with growing impatience until he apparently couldn't stand it anymore. "You're together. I get it. It's great."

Sandro frowned, hesitated, and then slowly brightened with relief. "It's great?"

"Well, it's great for you, because Sky's awesome. Not so great for her because you'll probably wreck it the way you wreck everything, but—"

She'd done a pretty good job thus far of letting father and son deal with their issues, but this was too big a test of her self-restraint.

"Nikolas," she began.

Sandro held up a hand to stop her, never taking his gaze away from Nikolas. "I'm human, son. I screw up. I admit it. But I always try my best." He hesitated, swallowing hard. "I'm still trying. Especially with you."

This confession seemed to throw Nikolas for a loop. He looked to the far wall, his jaw tightening, and then to his large bare feet as they poked out from under his flannel pajama bottoms. Then—finally, reluctantly—he looked back to his father.

And gave a single sharp and approving nod.

Chapter 12

Later that morning, Skylar was in the foyer, closing the front door after Mickey and Nikolas, who'd just gone to the market in Mickey's specially modified truck. The road had finally been cleared and they were badly in need of fresh groceries. Suddenly she heard distant strains of music so pure and haunting that it raised goose bumps on her arms and shivered down her spine.

She cocked her head, listening, as the music rose and coalesced into a melody: the plaintive strains of Beethoven's "Moonlight Sonata" coming from the study.

Lured like a sailor to a siren's song, she crept down the hallway and peered through the open door, not wanting to be seen in case she broke the spell.

The scene was extraordinary.

Sandro was there, but otherwise the surroundings bore no resemblance to what she'd walked in on her first night here. The shutters and drapes were all open, and the sun's bright rays streamed inside, making her squint against the illumination.

The piano was uncovered, its lid propped open, and Sandro sat at the bench with his head bent and his eyes closed. The lines of his face were tight, but not with strain. By now, they'd spent enough time making love for her to recognize rapture when she saw it, and it possessed him. Swayed through him. Changed him.

If she needed proof of how far he'd come since the night she had arrived, this was it, and it warmed her heart.

As though he sensed her presence, he opened his eyes, saw her and smiled.

"Come here." He opened his arms, beckoning her.

She was already on her way. "Don't stop. I didn't mean to interrupt you."

"It's okay."

"But it's been so long since you played."

"I'll play again."

"Promise?"

"As long as you keep inspiring me."

Taking her hand, he pulled her in front of him, and she sat on the keyboard with a discordant crunch. He eased between her thighs—she had jeans on now, alas—and, planting his hands on her butt, drew her closer. His expression as he looked up into her face was more intense than the sunlight.

"What?" she wondered, fascinated by this freer version of him, the one she'd always known was trapped inside somewhere. "Tell me."

"I never thought I'd be happy again."

She palmed his beloved face, which was prickly with stubble. "Are you saying you're happy with me?"

"You know I'm happy with you. Come here."

With a contented sigh, she eased down across his lap, straddling him and ignoring the way the keyboard pressed against her kidneys. Their mouths came together, but not before she whispered out *I love you* again.

She couldn't stop telling him how much she loved him.

They played, nipping and sucking, and then he slipped his tongue deep inside her mouth, making her hum with approval. His hands inched up under the hem of her sweater, and her skin burned. Sudden urgency made her writhe.

The floor, she thought, need rippling through her. No one else was home, and they could stretch out right here in front of the fire—

"Is this what I come home to?"

Startled by the interruption, they broke apart and looked around. Coming out of his sensual haze and moving with a soldier's reflexes, Sandro stood and shoved Skylar behind him, shielding her from the intruder.

A strange man stood there.

Tall, thin and haggard, he had the hollow-jawed, pale-skinned look of someone in the final throes of a terrible illness. He had skull-trimmed black hair and the scruff that came from several days of not shaving. His eyes were—

Jesus. His eyes.

They were shadowed and haunted, as though he'd seen every tragedy and cruelty the world had to offer, and yet they burned with the intensity of a zealot whose faith had been questioned.

Even though he didn't make any threatening moves and looked far too well dressed in his sweater and dark jeans to be a homeless person who'd broken in, those eyes scared her. So did the way his fingers flexed and clenched at his sides, and the way his upper lip peeled back on one side, giving him a fearsome sneer. His chest heaved as though all his rage was a single breath away from exploding out of him.

Police, she thought in that hushed moment.

They needed the police.

And then she looked again.

The heavy swoop of his black brows was familiar.

The straight line of his nose was familiar.

And the curve of his lips, even in their anger—that was familiar, too.

All of him was familiar, but the denial was stronger.

"No," she whispered, shaking her head.

"Tony?" Sandro reached out a hand and took a few

labored steps forward, as though the invisible air all around him had turned to sludge that held him back. *"Tony?"*

The man's face contorted with a killing fury.

"Is this what I come home to?" Tony roared.

The air whooshed out of Skylar's lungs, and a wave of sudden dizziness forced her to drop onto the piano bench. Pressing a hand to her chest, she gasped and managed several deep breaths, clinging to consciousness only by sheer force of will. The room swam, but she blinked it back into focus.

Sandro was frozen where he was now, that hand still outstretched. His face had turned to chalk. His voice was choked. "You're alive?"

That sneer widened. "Yeah. Sorry to disappoint you."

"But—how?" Sandro's voice rose and broke with emotion. "I don't understand. I don't—"

Tony shrugged irritably. "It's not that tricky. Remember the IED that blew our convoy and the bridge to kingdom come? Well, maybe you don't remember. Maybe it didn't make that big an impression on you, since you were in one of the lucky Humvees—"

"Tony!"

"—but my Humvee flipped off the bridge. And, let me tell you, it's a little hard to swim when you're loaded down with fifty pounds of armor and gear and—"

"Jesus," Sandro muttered, his face stark with horror.

"—so I said my prayers and got ready to meet my maker." Here, Tony paused to lean around Sandro and look at her. She could hardly see him through the shame and tears. "Are you listening to this, my beautiful ex-fiancée? Huh? Does my tragic little story move you at all? Given current events, I'm guessing not, but I thought you might like to hear about it."

Swiping at her eyes with one hand and gripping the bench for support with her free hand, she did a terrible job of pulling herself together. "Please, Tony—"

"So you can imagine my surprise when I woke up and I wasn't dead." He paused. "I only wished I was."

"Tony." Sandro's voice was now so heavy with dread that each word seemed to weigh a ton. "Where have you been this whole time?"

Tony stared at him. "Why, I've been enjoying the Taliban's first-class hospitality, of course. Where else would I have been? I did manage to escape, though. In case you were wondering."

Sandro dropped his head. His shoulders shook with quiet sobs so excruciating that it would have been a relief if Skylar had been able to cut off her own ears.

Tony's face twisted. "Why so sad, brother? Are you wishing you'd spent a little more time looking for me?"

"They did look for you—"

"They?" One of Tony's brows did a slow, cynical rise toward his hairline. "Not *you?*"

"I was injured, too, man—"

"Yeah? Broken finger? Tough break."

Sandro kept silent, apparently deciding that his internal injuries, bad as they'd been, wouldn't hold up against a lengthy spell as a prisoner of war.

In the harsh silence, no one spoke.

Sandro finally tried again. "When did you escape?"

Tony's expression was cold now. Flat. "About a month ago. I had to do the debriefing thing, and the medical evaluation thing, and now here I am."

"Why didn't anybody notify us?"

Tony bared a few of his teeth in a feral grin that would've done a wolf proud. "Well, now, that's a funny story. I asked folks to keep it quiet. I wanted the pleasure of surprising my family. Guess the surprise was on me, huh?"

Sandro shook his head and swiped his arm under his nose. He kept opening and closing his mouth, but nothing came out. Possibly because he didn't want to ask the obvious follow-up question.

"What did they do to you, man?"

"While you were doing Skylar, what was the Taliban doing to me?" Tony's accusatory gaze swung between the two of them, making Skylar flinch. "Is that the question? Do you really want to know?"

Sandro threw caution to the wind and stepped forward again, opening his arms to his brother. "I'm sorry, Tony. I'm sorry—"

Tony stiffened but stood his ground. "Stay away from me."

Sandro kept coming. "I missed you. You're my brother. I missed you—"

Still murmuring, Sandro grabbed Tony's shoulders and tried to pull him in for a hug; Tony jerked his arms free.

"Get off me."

"You're my brother—" Sandro reached again, which was one time too many.

Tony erupted, lashing out with the lethal force of a cobra strike. He delivered a brutal push to Sandro's chest that Skylar felt even from her safe distance. Sandro flew backward and hit the piano. The lid crashed, banging shut with endless reverberations so loud it was like being trapped inside a ringing gong.

Sandro dropped to his knees, wheezing.

Skylar cried out and reached for him, but Sandro pushed her hands aside, heaved himself onto unsteady legs, and reached for Tony. Again.

"You're my brother."

"You're *not* my brother!" Tony went nuclear, snarling and raging hard enough to turn his contorted face a blotchy purple. "You're *not* my brother! You thought *I* was dead? Well, *you're* dead!"

"You're my brother, Tony—"

"You're dead to me!" Tony shouted. "I will kill you!"

Skylar leaped between them. "Tony!" Grabbing his arms, she gave him a jerk that seemed to snap him out of some of the darkness, although he kept straining for Sandro as though he couldn't wait to make good on his threat. "Please! Please, Tony! Look at me!"

She jerked him again, and Tony's gaze wavered, dropping from Sandro to her.

Maybe she was taking her life into her hands, but a little voice told her to risk it. So she ever so slowly reached out to grip Tony's thin and grizzled cheeks between her hands and hold him while he panted.

"Tony."

That snapped him out of it.

He winced away from the contact, but she refused to let him go. When he finally looked into her eyes, she met his glare with gratitude. "Thank God," she said. "Thank God you're alive."

Tony stilled. And then his face crumpled. "Sky?"

"Thank God you're alive."

With a sharp breath, he snatched her into his arms and held on, burying his face into the hollow between her neck and shoulder and running his fingers through her hair. They swayed together and she squeezed his gaunt body as hard as she could for as long as he would let her, which wasn't long enough to quiet his shudders.

When he'd had enough, he abruptly thrust her aside and strode out without a backward glance at either of them, banging the door shut behind him.

Dread swallowed her up as she did a slow turn and met Sandro's shell-shocked gaze. She wanted to touch him, but he felt too far away, and it seemed impossible to get there from here.

"I have to go after him," she said helplessly.

It took him a long time to answer. "I know."

Gathering more courage than she'd known she had, she reached for his arm. It was a solid block of tension.

"This doesn't change anything, Sandro."

Sandro stared at her, his expression stark as he pulled free.

"It changes everything."

Skylar followed Tony upstairs, to the bedroom she knew had been his, and tapped quietly on the door. When he didn't answer, she slipped inside and discovered him out on the balcony, leaning against the railing. His gaze was riveted on the slate gray waves, which were hitting the beach one after the other, churning foam. Another storm was rolling in.

Or maybe it'd already arrived.

She came up behind him and was on the verge of calling his name—she didn't want to scare him—when he spoke without looking at her.

"My mother is dead," he said quietly.

"Yes," she admitted. "How did you know?"

He shot her a wry sidelong look. "I did a Google search for her. Some things don't change much."

Running a hand up his back, she squeezed his shoulder. "I'm sorry."

"My sister is a lawyer now. She married some guy I've never met."

"And she's pregnant."

"Yeah?" His head whipped around, his eyes wide with interest. "Google didn't tell me that."

"I think she's due any second."

Tony nodded, his gaze drifting back to the waves. "Good for her."

They stood together for a long time, the wind whipping between them. They didn't talk. Skylar wanted to say something—anything—but it was hard to think of a topic that wouldn't set him off.

After a while, he let her off the hook. "You look good, Sky."

"You look way too thin. Are you *okay?*"

His lip curled. "Define okay."

"Are you physically well?"

"Yeah. Now."

"What do you need? What can I do for you?"

A firm shake of his head dismissed this question. Maybe he thought he was beyond help. Or maybe it was hope he didn't believe in. "You can't help me."

"I want to try, Tony."

"You got a magic wand? Fairy dust? Genie in a bottle? 'Cause I'm thinking those are the only ways I'm going to get the lost parts of my life back, you know?"

There was no upbeat response to that, so she didn't try to manufacture one. "I know."

He turned to her again, his expression so bleak it might have been ripped from a post-apocalyptic landscape. "I guess I'm a selfish bastard."

"What? Why?"

"I didn't expect people to give up on me being alive so quickly. And I didn't think it would be this easy for people to go on without me."

"It wasn't easy. It's been terrible. Sandro has been sick with—"

"Sick?" His face twisted, hardening into something that scared her. Not that she thought he would hurt her; she was more afraid of what he was doing to himself. "Is that why you had your tongue down his throat a minute ago? Mouth-to-mouth?"

"Tony—"

"Why the crocodile tears, Sky? It looks like you and Sandro have been helping each other through the grief. Setting up house and—"

"We have not been setting up house! I arrived the other day to give him the papers relinquishing my share of the house to him. He was drinking, Tony. Staring at some of your possessions from the war—"

His brows flattened over his eyes.

"—your boots and tags and photos of you. He has a shrine going in the study. Did you notice that? The house was dark because he's been wallowing in his guilt and trying to keep it together enough to raise his son alone—"

"Ah, but he's not alone, is he? He's got you."

"You have to forgive him, Tony. You're not the only one who's been suffering—"

He leaned down in her face, lips pulled back in that sneer she was beginning to hate. "You're not seriously comparing being a POW to a case of survivor's guilt, are you?"

"No. Of course not. But you're home now and you're brothers. You need each other."

"Need?" Every hard syllable out of his mouth was like a whip's lash. "You want to talk about *need,* Sky? Well, I *needed* you, my beautiful fiancée, and I thought you *needed* me, but it turns out that all you *needed* was a Davies twin. Didn't matter much which one, did it?"

She deserved the accusation. Had even braced for it. But hearing it spat at her like that still filled her with hurt and shame.

"You and I weren't right, Tony. I should never have let things go so far between us, but I was—"

"What? Swept up in a little whirlwind romance with a soldier who was shipping out soon? Is that it?"

Why did it sound so ridiculous when he said it like that?

"I didn't mean to—"

"To what?" he roared. "To *what?* To fall in lust the second you met my brother at *our* engagement party? Because that's what happened, isn't it? Don't lie to me."

She struggled, helpless to explain something she still couldn't understand. "It was more than that—"

"Yeah? What was it, then?"

"I love him," she said simply. "If I'd cared about you the way I should have, I would never have been attracted to him in the first place. And that's why I'm so sorry. We should have always just stayed friends, Tony—"

"Is this you making me feel better? Because here I'd thought you loved *me.* That's why you said yes when I asked you to marry me. And now I find out you were just killing time until my brother came along?"

Could shame kill a person? It was crawling through her, drowning her in prickling heat. "I'm sorry," she said again. "I'm so sorry—"

"Sorry? Don't tell me that! That's not what I want to hear!"

"What, then? What should I do to—"

"You tell me why!" he shouted. "You tell me what he's got that I haven't got!"

"I don't want to hurt you—"

"That ship has sailed, sweetheart. And I need you to tell me so I can get past this. You owe me an explanation."

Yes, she did. Even if she didn't want to give it.

"It's his eyes. It's his tenderness and his vulnerability. It's the way I feel when I'm with him—"

"How is that?" he asked sharply.

"I'm not good with putting it in words," she tried.

"Tell me."

"I feel like I'm home when I'm with him. That's all."

She waited, certain that this fuzzy and probably unsatisfactory answer would set off another round of enraged shouting. It didn't. To her surprise, Tony's face eased, slackening with what looked like sudden understanding.

"But we're twins, Sky."

"I'm not saying it makes sense. But you and he are completely different."

They stared at each other for several beats, his expression slowly clearing.

At last his mouth softened into the scant beginnings of a smile. Her chest loosened with relief and a crazy kind of gratitude she'd never felt before.

"Tony," she began, her heart full of a thousand other apologies—for giving up on him, for not having more faith in him, for not being the woman he'd needed her to be—but he waved her to silence.

"We had some fun, didn't we? I didn't imagine it."

The implicit forgiveness choked her up, making her lips twist with repressed tears. This was a wonderful man standing here with her, even if he wasn't the wonderful man for her.

She took his face between her hands and stroked his gaunt cheeks. "We had a lot of fun."

Satisfied, he gave her a rueful nod, and a sweet charge of remembrance went through her. The next thing she knew, he'd cupped her cheeks and was leaning closer, his lids lowering.

"Goodbye, Sky," he murmured.

"Goodbye," she said, and tipped up her mouth to meet his.

The kiss was gentle, lingering, and so poignant that her heart ached with—

"Sorry to interrupt," Sandro said.

Oh, God.

Flustered, Sky broke away from Tony and turned to the doorway in time to meet the frigid blast of Sandro's gaze as he entered the room. Nikolas and Mickey followed behind and headed for Tony with glad cries.

She opened her mouth, ready to explain away the kiss, but Sandro wheeled around and was gone before she found her voice.

None of Sandro's usual coping mechanisms worked for him that night.

His study felt simultaneously overwhelming and stifling, as though a rain forest had been crammed into a cave, making it impossible for him to get his breath. The lamp in the corner was too bright, and yet the study was a crypt that threatened to suck the remaining pulse of life out of him. He couldn't sit still behind his desk, but pacing exhausted him. He longed for drunken oblivion, and should have been well on his way after four shots of vodka, but his mind remained stubbornly clear and the liquor became so disgusting that he couldn't get another drop down.

In fairness, though, it wasn't the liquor that disgusted him. He did that to himself.

Over in the corner, the piano mocked him, and he wished he had the energy to retrieve the mallet from the toolshed so he could come back and smash it.

Three emotions had him in a stranglehold, and he couldn't figure out which he felt the most.

Was it joy that his brother was alive and Sandro was, therefore, no longer a broken half of the missing whole?

Or was his old friend guilt reigning supreme, because not only had Sandro survived the attack, he'd left a man behind to suffer. Wasn't that worse than his brother's outright death would have been? Hell, when Tony was "dead," at least he was at peace. Now it turned out that Tony had been alive and imprisoned—which meant, let's face it, tortured—while Sandro endured such minor woe-is-me's as *Why does my son hate me?* and *What should I do with myself now that I'm not a soldier?*

So, yeah—guilt.

But there was an ugly new emotion in the mix tonight. Well, not *new,* exactly, but certainly more primitive and ferocious than it had ever been before.

Jealousy.

The images stalked him in all their high-def glory, slowly making him insane.

Skylar's undisguised emotion at realizing Tony was alive.

Skylar and Tony staring at each other with the inti-macy of former lovers...touching each other...falling into each other's arms.

Skylar running after Tony to console him.

Skylar...kissing Tony.

The jealousy twisted and writhed in his gut, seething and expanding until he could taste its foul bitterness on the back of his tongue.

He eyed the half-empty bottle of vodka. Hell, maybe it wasn't so nasty after all.

Topping off his shot glass, he raised it in a silent cheer to nothing and gulped it down. Gasping, he swiped a hand over the back of his mouth and resumed brooding.

The thing was, he'd examined the situation from every angle, and there was only one way it could turn out: badly. In life, he knew, there was always an action and a reaction. A sweet balanced by a bitter. A yin and a yang. And the price to be paid for Tony's miraculous return was simple.

Sky would go back to him.

It was inevitable.

Tony always recovered. He always landed on his feet and came out ahead. He was always the winner, a simple fact that Sandro should never have forgotten. Tony was back, he wanted Sky back and he would get Sky back. The only thing that remained to be seen was whether it happened sooner or later. Which of course depended on Sky's sense of duty. She'd claimed she'd loved Sandro, and maybe she really thought she did. But that was before. This was now. And she and Tony hadn't even waited half an hour before they'd fallen into each other's arms and picked up where they had left off.

So what was left for Sandro?

Nothing but the frigid emptiness he'd known before Skylar showed up on his doorstep.

Reaching for the vodka bottle, he poured again.

Suddenly Skylar strode in without knocking, came to stand on the other side of his desk, and stared down at him with her hands on her hips.

Her lips thinned. "What a surprise. You in the study. In the dark. Drinking by yourself. Who'd have thought?"

She had a fair point. "Like that old board game, Clue,

isn't it? Sandro in the study with the liquor. It's got a certain ring to it, don't you think?"

"Where were you at dinner?" she asked.

"In here, of course."

"Why weren't you with us?"

"Thanks for noticing I was gone. I wondered about that. I didn't want to ruin your little reunion scene."

"It's your reunion scene, too."

He shrugged. "Tony didn't seem that happy to see me."

"Tony's in shock."

Her obvious and ongoing concern for his sainted brother tightened everything inside him to the breaking point. If she'd been worried about a troubled stranger she'd met on, say, the train, he'd've admired her compassion. But since her shadowed face was for Tony, he wanted to rage and smash everything in sight. He hated himself for this pettiness, but he still felt it.

"Touching," he murmured, reaching for his glass. "Well, don't let me keep you."

She watched him, brows contracting. "He needs both of us now."

"Hmm. I'm betting he needs you more than he needs me. Cheers."

To his irritation, she interrupted his jeering little toast by snatching the glass from him and pouring its contents on his leather blotter. Then she slammed the glass back on the desk and wiped her hands on her jeans.

He glared up at her, waiting and hopped up on adrenaline.

"I'm sorry," she told him.

"For?"

"That kiss."

"Oh, was there a kiss?"

She shook her head, emitted a disbelieving little laugh, paced away from the desk and came right back, her face lined with determination. "Your sarcasm isn't going to get to me."

"No?"

"No. I know it's a defense mechanism. Plus, you're angry—"

Angry? She had ripped his heart out and then opined about him being *angry?*

Paralyzed by that poisonous jealousy, he couldn't hate her enough, much less choke out a response.

"—and you should be angry. I don't blame you."

"How generous."

She paused, nostrils flaring, and he could almost feel the reins of her temper slip through her fingers. "But it was a goodbye kiss, Sandro. That's all."

His face felt so hard and so hot that he could barely get his lips to move. "There was a lot more hello than goodbye in that kiss, Sky."

That caused the explosion he'd been hoping for and needing. With a harsh cry, she slammed her palms on the desk, making the bottle and glass jump.

"What are you doing? Why are you acting this way? You know I love you."

"Well, correct me if I'm wrong, but Tony knew you loved him, too, didn't he? Looks to me like there's still some of that loving going on even though you're trying to put a good face on it."

"'A good face'—*what?* What does that mean?"

He shrugged. "I suppose it means that you don't want to dump me right away."

Her jaw dropped with sudden comprehension. "Dump you? I'm not going to dump you!"

"Don't be too hasty. The perfect Davies twin is back and he still wants you. What's a girl to do? Decisions, decisions."

"There's no decision to make."

Hallelujah. She finally got it. Lunging across the desk, he caught her upper arm in a hard grip that made her yelp. "You're damn right there's no decision to make. He can't have you."

Several beats of excruciating silence passed, broken only by the harsh rattle of her shocked breath. "You can't seriously believe—" she began slowly and quietly, her voice cracking so badly that she had to stop and start again. "After the time we've spent together and the things we said and did together last night, you can't seriously question my feelings for you."

Oh, he had a lot of questions, but as far as he was concerned, there was only one answer. He tightened his grip on her arm.

"He can't have you."

"I'm leaving." With a low growl and glittering eyes, she snatched her arm free and pivoted for the open door. "I can't stand to look at you right now."

Chapter 13

A frozen moment passed, and all Sandro could do was stare after her and wonder how things had gotten this screwed up in such a head-spinningly short period of time. Then the panic set in.

"Skylar." Galvanized, he surged to his feet and hurried around his desk. If he could catch her before she—shit.

He stumbled through the doorway and into the hall, his feet tripped up by an indignant mewling fur ball that didn't appreciate the near loss of one of its nine lives. Perfect timing. Like he had time for kittens right now.

He grabbed the thing up by its scruff and hung on while it tried to squirm free, but then he caught a movement out of the corner of his eye. "Nikolas? Is that you?"

His son stepped from the shadows and hit a patch of

streaming moonlight from one of the hall windows. The sudden illumination let Sandro see the boy's stark expression. The poor kid was shell-shocked, and Sandro should know because he'd seen the look often enough in Afghanistan.

Things were, Sandro realized with a heart-contracting burst of clarity, about to get a hell of a lot worse.

The boy's blankness twisted and turned, knotting into anger fueled by fear. "Is she leaving?"

Sandro didn't know the answer to that question. He might be a sorry father, but he wasn't a liar, so he took the only other option and told the sad truth.

"I don't know."

Nikolas's jaw dropped. "You don't know? Are you shitting me right now?"

"Nikolas."

But it would take more than a firm voice to stop this volcanic burst of emotion that had been months, maybe years, in the making.

"You're unbelievable." The boy's deep voice boomed in the late night silence, reverberating off the walls and filling Sandro with a taste of his son's misery. "You take anything that's good and you screw it up! It's like a talent you have! Do you work at it, or what? I mean, seriously—how do you manage it?"

"I didn't—"

"Mom left. Sky's leaving. Hell, half the time I want to run away and get out of this gloomy-ass house! Why don't you go back to Afghanistan, man? Things were better when you were gone!"

Something was happening now that Sandro hadn't seen in a good ten years or more. Nikolas, a tough kid who took his lumps and didn't let much in life faze him, whether it was his mother's decision to walk out on the family or his expulsion from summer camp, started to cry.

Since he was equal parts man and boy now, the tears shamed him; Sandro could see it in the desperate way he swiped the back of his hand across his eyes and pressed his lips together while still struggling to talk. Suddenly all Sandro's turmoil about Tony's return and his future with Skylar—he would have a future with Skylar, and not even his irrational jealousy was going to ruin it—receded because his boy was in pain and needed whatever comfort he could offer.

"Why don't you leave, man? Why don't you get the hell out of here—"

"Nikolas." Holding the struggling kitten in a firm grip against his chest, Sandro reached out and grabbed the boy around the shoulders, reeling him in. Like the kitten, he flailed and resisted, trying to get away, but Sandro was bigger and his determination stronger. "Come here," he soothed, acting on pure paternal instinct, because God knew he was no Einstein when it came to dealing with tricky emotional scenes. "Come here. It's okay."

"Leave, man! Leave!"

"It's okay. It'll be okay."

To his astonishment, Nikolas wound down or wore himself out—Sandro couldn't tell which. But the next thing he knew, his son was submitting...relaxing...wrapping his wiry arms around Sandro's waist and holding on for dear life as he sobbed out all the turmoil of a teenager who'd lost a mother and gained a prickly relationship with a father who was learning how to be a dad.

"It's okay, buddy." Sandro kept up the mantra, even when his throat grew tight and hoarse and his own unhappiness threatened to choke him. "We're going to be okay. I'm not leaving you. I'm never leaving you again."

Eventually, some internal switch deep within Nikolas was flipped, and it was over. Having cried himself out, the boy had nothing left to focus on but his embarrassment, which seemed to be overwhelming. He gave Sandro's chest a hard push and broke free, hanging his head while he wiped his eyes and nose with the bottom edge of his T-shirt. Then he cleared his throat, shoved his hands deep into his pockets and shuffled his feet. He seemed to be waiting for something.

Sandro, feeling clumsy and inadequate and wishing he had a child psychologist on retainer to advise him during excruciating moments like these, cleared his throat, too.

The kitten continued to mewl.

This was one of those moments, wasn't it? Where a good father, one like, say, Cliff Huxtable, would offer a couple more words of comfort and wisdom.

Too bad there was no sign of Bill Cosby around here.

"So..." Since his throat still wasn't clear, he coughed

this time, opened his mouth and prayed for a word or two to come. "Things are, aah, kind of crazy around here right now, but they'll settle down."

"I doubt it," Nikolas grumbled, now studying his own toes. "You need to work things out with Sky. Don't blow it, man. You'll never do better than her. You know that, right?"

Out of the mouths of babes, eh?

"I know," Sandro admitted, and since they were discussing hard truths tonight, he decided to throw another one into the mix. "I'm not sure I deserve her, though."

Nikolas waved a hand, flapping away Sandro's biggest vulnerability. "Oh, you don't deserve her—"

"Thanks ever so much."

"But she's crazy about you. I don't think she'll want to leave here unless you drive her to it. So don't drive her to it. And give me the kitten. You're strangling her."

With that, he snatched the kitten—Leia, right?—away from Sandro and headed down the hall toward the kitchen, cradling her against his chest in a protective grip.

Leaving Sandro to wonder how to get himself out of the hole he'd dug with Sky.

About an hour later, after much pacing and moody ruminating, but no further drinking, Sandro lingered at the top of the stairs, trying to decide what to do.

His first option was to head down the west wing to Skylar's bedroom, where he'd spent the most incredible night of his life, prostrate himself at her feet and beg for her forgiveness for being a jealousy-racked jerk who couldn't handle even the vaguest suggestion that he might lose the happiness he'd only just found.

Option two was to head down the east wing to his own room, spend the night in a lonely and hard bed of his own making, wait until morning to commence the begging, and pray that cooler heads would prevail by the time the sun came up.

Option three was to head down the east wing to Tony's room and try to talk to him again, also begging forgiveness.

He hesitated in the dark hallway, trapped by indecision.

So what else was new? He was like Hamlet's black twin.

Maybe he should just go to bed and try it all again—

A distant howl cut through the silence, so raw and wounded that it chilled him like a dive into an icy northern lake. He whipped around, straining his ears against the night's utter stillness, and tried to isolate the source of all that pain. Sky? Nikolas? Mickey should be asleep in the guesthouse by now—

The noise came again, louder and more desperate this time, a shrill cry of unending pain. It went on for so long that he was able to get a bead on it.

Tony.

His body was already in action, operating on instinct and sprinting with a blind panic he hadn't felt since his feet touched American soil again. He banged through

Tony's door and into the room, searching wildly for the danger even though he knew, deep down, that he wouldn't find any.

A blast of frigid air hit him in the face, so cold that it burned his lungs on the inhale. What the—? The balcony doors were open, allowing the wind to whip up a frenzy of hard rain and flapping drapes. It was a meat locker in here, too icy for any human warmth to survive for long.

The moon's dim glow penetrated enough for him to see that there was nothing out of place. There was also no Tony. The giant four-poster bed loomed out of the shadows, but Tony wasn't in it and, judging by the smooth linens, had never been in it.

Listening with his entire being, he heard only absolute silence inside the room.

What the hell was going on here?

Pausing to click on the small lamp on top of the dresser, he strode to the balcony doors and snapped them shut. There. That was better. But where the hell was—

That eerie wail rose again, pleading and indecipherable. Sandro's flesh crawled with sympathetic anguish as his ears zeroed in on the source.

The sofa. The noise was coming from behind the sofa.

He was there in two strides, crouching at one end of the sofa, where it had been slid away from the wall just enough for an underweight man to stretch out on a nest of blankets. There was no pillow. Tony writhed, facedown, and struggled against the night terror that wouldn't let him go.

Jesus.

Determined to be gentle and not screw this up, Sandro reached out, touched his brother's thin shoulder and squeezed. There was no give in the tight muscles; he might as well have been touching reinforced steel. And despite the sub-zero temperature in here, Tony's flesh burned through the thin cotton of his T-shirt, generating enough heat to scorch Sandro's fingers.

Tony turned his head to the side, but didn't wake up.

Sandro hovered, just in case. Maybe Tony had settled down for now, but who knew? And how could he breathe with his face smothered in the blankets like that? What if Sandro didn't hear him the next time? What would happen—

Without warning, Tony doubled up, curling in on himself and heading for the fetal position, except that there wasn't room for it against the wall. His face twisted; his mouth opened in a silent scream.

"Talia," he cried. "Talia!"

Screw it. Throwing caution to the wind, Sandro grabbed both his shoulders and gave him a hard shake. "Tony. Wake up."

That seemed to do the trick. Tony surged upright into a sitting position, his back to the wall and his long legs bent against his chest. Wild-eyed, he looked around and tried to get his bearings, and then his expression coalesced into another one that Sandro had seen too many times before.

Ah, shit.

Tony lashed an arm out, reaching under the blankets. So did Sandro. A brief, grunting struggle followed, and Sandro clamped a hand down on Tony's wrist and held on for dear life. Tony, meanwhile, was brandishing a hunting knife.

They fought, the blade glinting at face level between them. Since Sandro didn't plan to kill or be killed in a crazy domestic accident after they'd both survived the war and come home in one piece, Sandro squeezed Tony's wrist even harder.

"Tony! Wake up! It's me, Sandro!"

Tony blinked, some of the snarl leaving his face. "Sandro?"

"Yeah, idiot. It's your brother. So don't kill me, okay?"

Tony's expression cleared and his eyes came into focus. *"Sandro."*

"You okay?" Sandro asked warily.

Tony ran his free hand over the top of his head. "Yeah."

"Maybe you could drop the blade."

Tony, to his great relief, dropped it.

Feeling much better, Sandro surged to his feet and extended a hand. Tony took it in a hard grip. Sandro gave him a tug, and the next thing he knew, Tony was on his feet but still in motion.

They came together in one of those punishing, backslapping hugs that was more a test of a person's pain threshold than a display of affection. Swaying and too choked on their mutual emotional torment to manage any words, they held each other upright.

It wasn't until this precise moment of reunion that Sandro realized how much he'd missed this other half of himself, and how sick he'd been without him.

"I'm sorry, man," he said gruffly, his face wet with the kind of tears that a soldier hated to cry. He squeezed the back of Tony's neck, anchoring him here, to his house and his family, where he belonged. "I'm sorry. I'm sorry—"

The only consolation was that Tony was also having problems with eye leakage. "I missed you, you punk," Tony told him, giving his cheek a hard kiss. "I missed you."

Overcome, Sandro did the only manly thing left, which was to make a joke and hope they could pretend this interlude never happened. "Yeah, okay, don't get crazy," he said, breaking free and turning away.

"I didn't dismiss you, soldier."

Lashing out, Tony hooked him around the neck and bent him up in the same headlock he'd been using on him since they were three. Sandro struggled, but the truth was, it felt good.

Really, really good.

"Okay." Tony turned him loose with a rough shove that tumbled Sandro onto the sofa. "Now you're dismissed."

He collapsed beside him and they sat there together, breathless and a little stunned by this turn of events.

"Night terrors, eh?" Sandro asked after a while.

Tony shrugged. "It's the war that keeps on giving."

Sandro hesitated, not wanting to set anything off again but determined to get his brother the help he needed.

"Are you, aah—"

"Seeing anybody?" Tony finished for him. "Taking anything? Yeah. This is better, actually. If you can believe it."

"It takes time."

"Time," Tony echoed dully. "Yeah."

"What'll you do?"

Another shrug. "Maybe take a stab at the auction business. Listen—" he swung around, turning to face Sandro on the sofa and picking his words carefully "—about Skylar—"

A few minutes of brotherly reconciliation, it turned out, did not kill, or even maim, the roaring jealousy inside Sandro's chest. He felt his jaw tighten into finely tuned piano wire.

"I'm not giving her up," he said flatly. "She belongs with me."

Judging by the sudden flash of annoyance in Tony's eyes, he didn't appreciate the tone, but that was too freaking bad. They needed to get a few things straight between them, and Skylar was not a gray area. He squared his shoulders, gearing up for a battle, but Tony surprised him.

"Yeah, she does."

"Just so we're clear—wait, *what?*"

"If you're pulling that tough-guy shit with me, then this conversation's over. Let me know."

"Fine." With a lot of difficulty, Sandro reined in his possessive streak and locked it in its cage. "Don't keep me in suspense."

Tony nodded, looking mollified, but when he opened his mouth again, the words didn't come. The moment stretched, heading into awkward territory. Sandro waited, studying his knees, and pretended he didn't see the way Tony's cheeks flooded with color or the way his nostrils flared.

"The thing is," Tony said finally, "she was never... like that...with me."

Thunderstruck, Sandro stared at him and wondered if he was saying what he thought he was saying.

"When I walked in on... Jesus. Don't make me say it, man."

Sandro thought about the way Skylar melted down in his arms and the way she looked at him. The way she'd always looked at him. How she'd been saying, over and over again, how much she loved him.

And he got it.

He also understood something else with stark clarity: Tony was a million times the man Sandro was. Because there was no way—no way in a thousand lifetimes and a million universes—that he could ever stand aside and wish Skylar happiness with another man.

"Thanks," he said gruffly. "I, aah—thanks."

Tony's gaze narrowed with warning. "She loves

you, man. So you better take good care of her so I don't change my mind about wanting her back."

Sandro now knew that it didn't matter what Tony wanted. Skylar's choice was the important thing here, and they all knew she'd picked Sandro.

"I plan to treat her like a queen," Sandro assured him. "Now I have a question for you."

Tony raised a brow, looking wary.

"Who's Talia?" Sandro asked.

Slippers, Skylar remembered. She needed her slippers, which she'd kicked under the bed the other night. Oh, and also the blue sweater she'd worn the other day, which was probably still draped over the back of the armchair. So she'd have to get that when she went downstairs. She eyeballed her mostly packed suitcase, which was open on the bed, and checked the time: five thirty-three. In the morning.

Which was a tad too early to head to the airport for her three-thirty flight.

The sensible thing to do, since it was still dark outside, would be to go back to bed and try to get some sleep. Too bad she wasn't in a sensible mood. It was more like a scream-in-frustration-and-rip-her-hair-out-by-the-roots-and-then-smash-something sort of mood.

And underneath all that? Blinding terror.

Because despite all the progress she'd made and the relationship she'd thought they were building, Sandro was still trapped by his guilt and shackled to his honor. Now that Tony was alive—and thank God for that!—

wasn't it only a matter of time before he dumped her? What would she do then? How would she recover when he smashed her heart to dust?

Tony, meanwhile, was a train wreck in progress; she knew it. Who would help him once she ran away? She didn't delude herself about this whole packed-suitcase thing. She was turning tail and running, and it really chapped her hide, because she wasn't a coward. Not normally, anyway.

If she left, how could she and Sandro ever work things out?

How would they—

Someone tapped quietly on her door.

She stilled. Deep inside her chest, her heart did several cartwheeling backflips.

She was still frozen with indecision when Sandro, wearing a T-shirt and flannel pajama bottoms, slipped inside the room and closed the door, shutting them in together with so many seething emotions that Skylar was sure she'd explode.

He looked just like she felt: wired and exhausted. Dark circles ringed his eyes, and his face had tightened with tension, making him all sharp edges and intense eyes. He didn't smile.

"I need to tell you something," he told her.

Here it came. The big kiss-off, filled with noble sprinklings about what he could or could not do as an honorable brother and blah, blah, blah. Anger surged, because she was pretty sure nothing she could say right now would change his mind, but she damn sure wasn't going to go down quietly, packed suitcase or no.

"I can't believe you're going to throw our whole relationship away because of a goodbye kiss. I mean, I know how it probably looked, but it didn't mean anything and I just don't understand—"

"I'm in love with you."

"—how you can think that there's still anything between me and Tony. I mean, come on. Think about it. We had our chance and it didn't—"

"And I want you to unpack all your stuff and stay here with me."

"—work out, so you have to know that I—wait, *what?* What did you say?"

He stepped closer, his glittering gaze locked with hers. She held her breath, not wanting to miss it this time.

"I'm in love with you," he said slowly. "Stay with me."

Oh, God.

One of her shaky hands flew up to cover her heart and keep it from bursting out of her chest. "You—you're in love with me?"

"You know I am."

That was a great start, but with him it was only half the battle.

"And you know I love you, right? *You.*"

Those familiar dark shadows tried to float across his face, but he blinked them away. She watched, disbelieving, as a smile curled one side of his mouth.

"After my performance earlier? I'm not sure you should."

"Sandro."

"Come here."

She went and he caught her up, lifting her off her feet until only her toes skimmed the floor. She locked her arms around his neck and held tight, home where she belonged and determined to stay there. He hung on to her waist and buried his face in the curve where her shoulder met her neck, breathing her like the air. They might have stayed like that forever, but, as always, the heat between them burned too bright to be ignored.

"I need you," he told her.

"I know."

"Now." He swung her around and laid her across the bed, his face hard and dark as he swept his T-shirt over his head, dropped it to the floor and went to work on his pajama bottoms. Straightening, he revealed a jutting erection that was full and thick, which was good because she was more than ready.

He crawled onto the bed and loomed over her, finding his place in the cradle between her open thighs and yanking her panties down her legs. "Now."

"I know."

She'd already slithered out of her silky robe and reached for him, her back arching and hips thrusting with no conscious command from her brain. It had always been this way with him, since that first time they laid eyes on each other. Heat. Instinct. Home. Nothing else was important.

A quick stroke with his fingers told him how hot she was and made his eyes roll closed with what looked like ecstasy. She waited, her breath stalled in her throat, but instead of the insistent surge of his member, she felt those talented fingers again, and he touched her there, right there—

"Sandro, please." She writhed, not sure if she wanted him to stop or not. "I want you inside me when I come."

He shrugged, flashing a hint of a smile that was more wicked than remorseful. "I don't think you can wait."

He was right. Those slick fingers glided slowly… slowly…and she came with a sharp cry of relief and pleasure.

There was no chance to catch her breath. "Sandro," she said. "Sandro, please—"

"I really like the sound of that." Hooking an elbow behind one of her knees, he spread her wide and drove deep inside her body with a single thrust.

"Hmm… What?" she gasped, trying to focus against the spiraling tension as it pooled, again, in her engorged sex. "Hearing me beg?"

"Hearing you come."

"Oh, good. Because you're about to hear it again."

"Good deal."

Dipping his head, he caught her mouth beneath his, surging with his tongue in time to the swiveling of his hips.

She moaned and arched back into the pillows, her face

twisting with pleasure. "Hmm, yeah… Right there…ah, yeah, right there."

"Here?"

He worked her harder, just the way she needed, and she opened her eyes, focusing on the straining cords in his neck, the sweat across his forehead and the glitter in his half-closed eyes.

"Tell me," she said.

"What? How crazy I am about you?"

"That you love me."

"I love you."

"And you've always loved me."

His lips thinned, and he faltered, choked with sudden emotion. "I've always loved you. Always."

"And you always will."

He blinked furiously, but his eyes overflowed. A single tear fell, splashing her cheek, and her heart swelled beyond anything she thought she could survive.

"And I always will," he whispered.

Later, as they lay twined together under the downy comforter, their sweat-slicked bodies cooling as their breath evened out, Sandro pressed her closer to his side and traced lazy circles on her back.

"You know," he warned her, "the Davies family is in a state of, aah—"

"Upheaval?"

"I was going to say chaos, but, yeah, let's go with upheaval. Nikolas and I still have issues to work out, and most days he's not even talking to me."

"True."

"Tony's in bad shape. He's having nightmares and he told me a little bit about what they did to him when—"

Jesus. He couldn't finish.

Skylar, of course, understood. She nuzzled closer, pressing a sweet kiss to his chest. "I understand."

"He's going to need help."

"I know."

"From both of us."

She raised her head, studying him with worried eyes. "Are you okay with that?"

"Yes," he said honestly.

She dimpled. "Good."

"And we're going to call my sister Arianna in a little while. Let her know he's still alive. So I imagine the second that she pops that baby—"

"Wow. You're so eloquent."

"—she and her husband and the baby are going to show up on our doorstep."

"Good to know."

"Plus, we've got Mickey rolling around here, bossing us around and generally being a sarcastic pain in the ass."

"Right."

"And there's a growing menagerie of pets that I don't know what to do with."

"Good thing you know a vet, right?"

He rolled over, easing her beneath him so he could see her face for this next part. "So the point I'm making," he told her, "is that when you marry me, you'll be marrying all of this. Got it?"

She smiled, her eyes tearing up. "Oh, yeah. I got it."

He'd thought he'd reached the outer limits of his happiness with Skylar already, but he was, as usual, wrong. Joy swelled in his chest, threatening to split him open down the middle.

"Is that a yes?"

"It's a yes," she said. "I can't wait to see what further adventures the Davies family has in store for me."

* * * * *